The Best Goodbye

ALSO BY ABBI GLINES

In publication order by series

The Rosemary Beach series
Fallen Too Far
Never Too Far
Forever Too Far
Twisted Perfection
Simple Perfection
Take a Chance
Rush Too Far
One More Chance
You Were Mine
Kiro's Emily (novella)
When I'm Gone
When You're Back

The Sea Breeze Series
Breathe
Because of Low
While It Lasts
Just for Now
Sometimes It Lasts
Misbehaving
Bad for You
Hold on Tight

The Vincent Boys Series
The Vincent Boys
The Vincent Brothers

The Existence Series
Existence
Predestined
Ceaseless

The Best Goodbye

A Rosemary Beach Novel

Abbi Glines

ATRIA PAPERBACK

New York • London • Toronto • Sydney • New Delhi

ATRIA PAPERBACK

An Imprint of Simon & Schuster, Inc.
1230 Avenue of the Americas
New York, NY 10020

This book is a work of fiction. Any references to historical events, real people, or real places are used fictitiously. Other names, characters, places, and events are products of the author's imagination, and any resemblance to actual events or places or persons living or dead is entirely coincidental.

First Atria Paperback edition December 2015

ATRIA PAPERBACK and colophon are trademarks of Simon & Schuster, Inc.

For information about special discounts for bulk purchases, please contact Simon & Schuster Special Sales at 1-866-506-1949 or business@simonandschuster.com.

The Simon & Schuster Speakers Bureau can bring authors to your live event. For more information or to book an event, contact the Simon & Schuster Speakers Bureau at 1-866-248-3049 or visit our website at www.simonspeakers.com.

Manufactured in the United States of America

10 9 8 7 6 5 4 3 2

Library of Congress Cataloging-in-Publication Data is available.

ISBN 978-1-5011-1531-8
ISBN 978-1-5011-1538-7 (ebook)

To Heather Howell, for always making me laugh until my side hurts, having my back in all things, and coming along in my life when I needed someone as badass as you by my side. Love you lots, girl.

The Best Goodbye

Rose

Being short sucks. There was never a time in my life when I thought, *Gee, being short is awesome.* Not once. I could never reach things in high-up places. Which was what was happening now. I'd been sent by Elle to unpack the glasses and line them up on the shelves behind the bar, but I was struggling more than I cared to admit.

I wasn't a fan of the head server. She was gorgeous and mean, not to mention tall. She had no idea how hard it was for someone who was only five foot four to balance on a bar stool on her tiptoes with her hands full of glasses. Or maybe she did know, and she was doing this just to be cruel.

Leaning forward, I slipped another glass safely into one of the slots built into the wall for just this purpose. The stool wobbled, and I stilled, holding my breath. Easing back slowly, I managed to keep my balance. Only two more boxes to unpack, I thought, wishing that each box didn't hold ten glasses.

"You break those glasses, and the cost comes out of your paycheck. I don't have room in the budget for broken inventory," a deep voice drawled behind me. I knew that voice. I didn't hear it often, but when I did, it was usually annoyed with me.

Once, it hadn't been that way. Once, that voice had eased my fears, protected me, and given me a safe place to go. Now all I got were cold, detached words from him. I kept thinking the pain would ease up eventually. But it never did.

Time had changed both of us. Instead of loving him until I was breathless, I just wanted to slap his handsome face and leave town.

"Get down, Rose," River ordered harshly. "Go do something useful. I'll get someone who can manage this."

At least he remembered my name this time. Last week, he had referred to me as Rachel, Daisy, and Rhonda on three separate occasions. My constant corrections must have stuck. I got that the man had a restaurant full of new employees, and the stress of the grand opening in just two weeks' time was weighing on him. But still. The boy I once knew had been kind, thoughtful, and a hero. My hero.

At some point over the past ten years, River had changed his name to Captain and had become hard. Untouchable. Even his girlfriend, the oh-so-nice Elle, didn't seem to have access to a softer side of River. The side I'd once known best. No one had that. I didn't believe it existed anymore.

"Elle told me to put the glasses away," I said, jumping down from the stool and standing up as straight as I could. River was well over six foot two now, and he'd always towered over me. Even when we were sixteen.

He didn't comment on that. Instead, he nodded toward the kitchen. "Brad needs help with the cooking supplies that just came in. Go help him. I'll find someone who isn't vertically challenged to finish this."

My face flushed hot from embarrassment. It wasn't like I'd messed up or broken anything. I had done just fine. I was doing the job slowly, but I was getting it done.

"I'm fine. My height isn't affecting my ability to do this job, if that's what you mean," I snapped at him.

He didn't even glance back at me as he sauntered toward the door. "We open in two weeks. I'd like the glasses to be up by then." He walked out.

"Jerk," I muttered. I had a good mind to finish putting those glasses up myself anyway. But with my luck, I'd end up breaking an entire box of them. I couldn't afford to lose this job. I had packed up my life and come down to Rosemary Beach, Florida, once I found out that this was where I could find River. I hadn't thought past that. I had searched for him for years with no luck.

This lead had been the first real one I'd had. So I'd taken it. Getting this job had been easier than I thought, and I needed it. This town wasn't big, and it was hard to find employment. The house I'd found for rent was just outside the town limits— and it was tiny—but it was safe and affordable. That was all we needed.

We were living in the guest house of one of the massive beach homes that lined the shore. The only resident in the main house was an elderly lady, Diana Baylor, who seemed thrilled to have us right outside her back door. It was a good fit for all of us.

Without this job, I would have no reason to get close to River. And I had a mission. One I was no longer so sure of. I had to remind myself that I wasn't doing this for me. My needs and desires had taken a backseat nine years ago when Ann Frances had entered the world and become my reason for living.

The day Franny had turned five, she'd asked for one thing: to meet her father. Every year since then, that was all she ever asked for, on her birthday and on Christmas Day, without fail. She wanted to know her dad like her friends knew theirs. I'd made excuses and tried to compensate for the fact that she only had me. But then I had begun looking for the boy I had loved so much, then one I'd sacrificed everything for to keep him safe.

Looking back, I wondered if my sacrifice was a mistake. Franny's plea to meet her father made me feel I'd failed her while trying to save River. But I'd been a kid myself then, with choices to make that affected the only people in the world I loved.

"Are you going to finish the job I gave you or stand there and do nothing?" Elle's voice snapped me out of my thoughts. Her long dark hair was draped over her shoulders, and those catlike green eyes of hers glared at me. I wasn't sure why she had decided to hate me, but she had.

"Captain told me to stop and help Brad in the kitchen," I replied, trying not to let my dislike for her lace through my tone. If she complained to River, I was sure he'd fire me.

Elle was one of the biggest obstacles to my plan. I didn't want anyone so vicious in Franny's world. As much as my daughter wanted to know her father, I had to decide if that man was worthy of Franny. Sadly, I'd found after two weeks of working for him that he wasn't exactly measuring up. I wasn't sure I would ever be able to fulfill my daughter's one request.

"Fine. Then go. You're wasting time. We have things to do," she ordered, pointing toward the kitchen as if I didn't know where it was.

With a sharp nod, I headed that way. No reason to stay in her presence any longer than necessary.

Captain

Nothing was running on schedule. We should have been closer to opening than we were, but I'd waited too long to hire the full staff. That mistake was on me. But now I was beginning to question my choice of employees. Fixing what was wrong with a restaurant was one thing; opening a whole new joint was another. This wasn't what I wanted to do with the rest of my life, and I was questioning how much effort I wanted to pour into this place.

I was done with my past, but facing the future wasn't proving to be easy or promising. Maybe I needed a new direction. Once this place was up and running, I'd leave it in someone else's hands to operate and go find a fishing town somewhere with a bar on a pier that I could buy. Running a bar for a bunch of local fishermen seemed more my speed.

Getting this place open and running successfully had to happen first. Not just because I owed it to Arthur Stout, the owner, but because I always finished what I started. What Arthur was paying me would allow me to find that bar on a pier so I could finally enjoy the easy life.

"We need to fire that redhead. She's not cut out for this," Elle announced, as she walked into my office.

I didn't have to ask her who she was referring to; I already knew. Rose Henderson was petite, with curves that could stop traffic and the face of an angel. The cute pair of glasses she wore didn't hinder her looks, either; they just made her eyes stand out. That only made Elle hate her more. She didn't like competition, and I could tell she saw Rose as a threat. Not because I'd given her any reason but because every male who worked here clearly noticed Rose. She was hard to miss.

"Which redhead would that be?" I asked, not looking up from my unfilled orders.

"The short one. The one who can't do shit. I told her to put those bar glasses away, and she complained to you. I'm head server, Captain. She can't go over my head."

I'd hired Elle as head server because she'd come highly recommended by someone Arthur trusted. I agreed to it soon after meeting and interviewing her. Fucking her in my office the next day hadn't been planned, but she'd come on to me hard, and she was hot. I didn't see an issue with it. I liked tall, willowy women. She fit the bill. But she also confused the fact that she was sleeping in my bed with having some kind of control over me, and I needed to fix that.

"*We* didn't hire Rose, Elle. I did. And *we* won't be firing anyone. She didn't go over your head. She couldn't reach the shelves. She was going to fall and break something. I gave her something else to do."

Although I wasn't looking up at her, I could feel her frustration building. She didn't like my answer. Elle had a bit of a control problem. But she gave excellent head.

"I don't want her here." She pouted.

Finally, I looked up at her. She had her full lips puckered

out like she was going to cry. It would have looked ridiculous, but she knew how to pull it off in just the right way. Pushing back from the table, I patted my thigh. "Come here, Elle," I demanded, keeping my face serious.

She moved slowly around my desk, slipping her bottom lip between her teeth. Excitement flared in her eyes. That was the one thing I could count on. If I needed to calm Elle down, sex would do it.

"If you want to use that sexy mouth to turn me on, then you need to use it to get me off," I told her when she stopped in front of me.

"Where do you want me?" she asked breathlessly.

"On your knees," I ordered. She went down quickly and began to unbuckle my pants.

I wrapped a strand of her dark hair around my finger and let the silky texture tease me while she tugged my jeans down, then my boxers, until my cock was in her hands.

"As far down your throat as you can take it," I told her, as I started caressing her exposed neck.

She made a whimpering sound that went straight to my dick. Bending her head, she pulled me into her mouth like a fucking vacuum, and I tilted my head back and groaned. I needed this today. Best stress reliever there was.

"That's it, baby, suck it hard," I encouraged her, placing a hand on the back of her head and pushing her gently so that I slid farther down her throat.

The gagging noise only made me hotter. I loved it when she choked around my dick.

"Good girl. So fucking good." I praised her, knowing she'd

only get better with the praise. "Suck that dick. Deeper, baby. So good."

A knock on my office door caused her to freeze, but I held her head still so she couldn't pull away.

"I'm busy. Go away," I called out.

When the person said nothing, I patted her head for her to finish. Which she did.

An hour after Elle left my office, I headed to the kitchen to see if Brad had gotten everything in his order. My stress levels were down, and Elle seemed more secure and less anxious to get rid of Rose. Reminding Elle that she was the one I was fucking had done wonders for her attitude.

Laughter was the first thing I heard when I walked into the kitchen, Brad's deep chuckle followed by a feminine one. I followed the sound to the back of the kitchen and found Brad covered in what looked like flour, while Rose held her stomach and laughed to the point of breathlessness. Rose turned to look at me.

A tightness in my chest hit me as her eyes danced with laughter. The clear blue of them was familiar, but it was more than that. It was as if I'd seen her laugh before. Heard her laugh. Watching her made my chest ache in a way that didn't make sense. As if I . . . missed her. But I didn't even know her.

All too soon, her smile fell, and she wiped away the tears that had formed from laughing so hard. She shifted her gaze to Brad. I made her nervous, but then I'd never been nice to her, exactly. She was just an employee I'd hired. I'd be leaving soon enough. I wasn't here to make friends.

"Sorry, boss. I was reaching for a box on that shelf over there, and a bag of flour fell over, and, well, you can see what happened," Brad explained, still chuckling. I tore my gaze from Rose and looked at Brad. He winked at her and began a futile attempt to dust the flour off. He needed a shower. I wouldn't mind if he put some distance between himself and Rose.

Rose

Franny's blond curls bounced as she ran from the edge of the water toward me. Mrs. Baylor sat under an oak tree with a fruity drink in her hand and a wide-brimmed straw hat on her head. The two of them had bonded, and Mrs. Baylor had offered to watch Franny while I worked. She said it gave her something to do and someone to spend time with.

Franny had never had any kind of grandparent in her life, but she wanted a family. It was something she'd always noticed about other kids—the way they were surrounded by a mom, a dad, siblings, grandparents, cousins, aunts and uncles— and she longed for the same thing. But it was the one thing I couldn't give her, because I hadn't had a family, either. As a foster child from the time I was five years old until I ran away at sixteen, I only had one person in my life whom I considered family. The only family Franny had, too: River.

She had my hair, or at least my natural color, and my eyes, and bless her heart, she seemed to have inherited my short stature, too. The only thing about her that wasn't a complete replica of me was her complexion. I was fair, while Franny turned a golden brown from being out in the sun, even for just a little while. She got that from her father. She also had his sense of humor and his smile. But those were things only a mother would notice. To everyone else, she was just like me.

"I caught a fish, Mommy! A real live fish. Except I had to take the hook out of its mouth and throw it back before it died. I didn't want to kill it. I hope the hook didn't hurt it too badly. Mrs. Diana said it was OK. Fish are supposed to be eaten, but I wanted it to find its family. They could have been missing her."

Franny hardly took a breath in her long explanation, then she threw her arms around my waist and hugged me tightly. "I missed you today, but we had fun. We made chocolate fudge brownies."

I bent down to kiss the top of her head and turned to look over at Mrs. Baylor. She smiled warmly and stood up. The long strapless dress she wore danced in the wind around her legs as she walked toward us. She always looked so put together and glamorous.

"How was work today, Rose?" she asked.

"Good, thank you," I replied, smiling. "I hear the two of you had a full day of fun."

Mrs. Baylor grinned at Franny fondly. "This one makes the days brighter. But a fisherman she is not."

Franny giggled and tugged on my hand. "Let's go inside and have some brownies and milk."

"Yes, let's all spoil our dinner with the decadence of chocolate fudge," Mrs. Baylor agreed, gesturing toward the main house. She never seemed anxious for us to go back to our own cottage. I wondered if she was going to miss Franny once school started next week. They had gotten so close. At least I knew that when Franny got off the school bus every day, she'd have a treat and a hug waiting for her.

It made everything so much easier. I had struggled with the decision to leave Oklahoma, where we were settled in and safe. Franny had friends there, and my job as the secretary at her school had kept me close to her. Moving here had been a major leap for us, but I had done it for Franny. And deep down, I had done it for River.

I didn't want to regret this decision, although the more I saw of River, the more I wished we had stayed in Oklahoma.

Fourteen years ago

Another foster home. I didn't get attached to any of them. I'd stopped wishing for a family years ago. Now I just hoped that no one would hurt me and that I'd get fed every day. Because I knew what being hurt and not getting fed felt like.

Cora stood beside me, with her hard frown and tense stance. She didn't expect me to last here, either. We had been through this before. I'd been moved from home to home over the past eight years, ever since my mother had left me in a grocery-store parking lot. Cora Harper was my social worker and had been in charge of placing me in each new home.

"You be good here, Addison. Don't argue with them. Don't complain. When you're told to do something, then do it. Get good grades, and no fighting in school. This home could be the one for you. They want a daughter. You just have to be good."

I was always good. At least, I tried to be. I didn't argue. I asked for food when my stomach hurt because I was hungry, and I only got into a fight that one time at school because the other girl had pushed me down and called me names. I tried my best to be good. I just realized that my best wasn't good enough. I couldn't hope it would be different here.

"Yes, ma'am," I replied politely.

Cora glanced down at me and let out a small sigh. "You're a beautiful child. If you'd just act right, you'd find a home you could stay in."

I had the urge to tell her that I did act right. It was on the tip of my tongue, but I bit it back and only nodded. "Yes, ma'am," I replied again.

I followed Cora up the steps to the pretty yellow house with a big white porch wrapped around it. I liked the look of this place. The other houses I had lived in didn't look anything like this. They were usually old and smelled funny.

Before Cora could knock on the door, it opened slowly. A tall boy stood there. He had blond hair that was a little too long and shaggy. His green eyes went from Cora to me. Then he frowned. I had never really seen a boy I thought was beautiful until now, and he was frowning at me. I hadn't even messed up yet.

"You're little. Thought you were my age," he said, staring at me.

I hated being called short. Everyone talked about me being small for my age. I got teased about it at school enough. Straightening my shoulders, I tried to stand taller. "Maybe you're just too tall," I snapped in response.

Cora's hand wrapped around my shoulder, and she squeezed so hard I winced. Her long nails bit into my skin, reminding me that I had to make this work. If I didn't, I would be taken to a girls' home next, and I knew the nightmares that happened there. I'd heard stories.

"Sorry," I murmured through the pain in my shoulder, where Cora hadn't let go of me.

"Let her go. You're hurting her," the boy said angrily, jerking my attention back up to his handsome face. He was glaring at Cora like he was ready to remove her hand himself. "Jesus, she's tiny. You don't have to squeeze the hell out of her," he said, scowling.

"River Kipling! Watch your language," a voice called out, just before the figure of the woman who would become my worst enemy filled the doorway.

Captain

My eyes flew open, and I threw off the blanket, bolting up and sliding to the edge of the bed before taking a deep breath. I was covered in cold sweat, and my heart was still pounding. This dream was one I knew well, but it had been a while since I'd had it. From the time I was sixteen, I'd been fighting one demon—the one that tore my heart out and never gave it back again.

Fucking death. I had killed men. So many men. Men who deserved to die. Men who had abused children. Men who didn't belong on this earth. With each one, I was saving *her*. The one I had failed. The one I hadn't been able to save. I had tried to conquer that horror in so many ways, yet ten years later, I still dreamed about her. On other nights, I dreamed about how I had lost her. How I hadn't been strong enough to save her. Screwing my eyes shut, I inhaled deeply and buried my face in my hands. Each breath burned, and my chest cracked open.

Addy's beautiful face looking up at me, smiling, while her blond hair danced around her in the wind. The image made me feel complete, but it was just a tease. A sweet memory. One of the last memories I had of her. But the dream always turned so quickly. Blood everywhere. Addy in a pool of it, and all I could see was her. The woman who had raised me laughing as she watched Addy die. I screamed each time, but I was unable to get near her. I was frozen. Unable to save her in the dream or even to hold her.

She had been my soul mate. My other half. Even when we were kids, I had known she was the best friend I'd ever have. It hadn't taken long for me to realize I loved her. Once, I feared I loved her too much.

Thinking about Addy hurt more than I could describe. I kept waiting for it to ease, for the day when I would be able to think of our time together with a smile. But I knew I'd never do that. She had lost her life because of me. So beautiful and delicate. All I had ever wanted to do was protect her and hold her close.

I had to shake this before I went to work. It had been months since I'd dreamed of Addy. Usually, it was because something spurred a memory. I wasn't sure what it was this time. Why she was back in my dreams, which so often turned into nightmares. But something was making me think of her.

It wasn't Elle. That much I was sure of. I was careful never to date anyone who reminded me of Addy. Blondes and petite women were off my radar. I had tried that once, and the memories had hit me so hard I almost broke down and went for professional help. Memories of her had been killing me slowly, for a while. Making me wish I'd gone with her. Life seemed pointless without her smile.

But I was tougher than that, and I had found a way to live.

Even if that way had been to take the lives of others. My past wasn't something I regretted, though. I had done what needed to be done to save myself and stop perverts from hurting other children. It wasn't legal, but I wasn't one to give a shit about the law.

I got up and went to take a shower and find a way to push the memories back into the recesses of my mind.

Two hours later, when I walked into my office, Major Colt was sitting on the sofa across from my desk, with that ever-present smirk on his face. If the guy wasn't so good at what he did, I wouldn't have hooked him up with Benedetto DeCarlo. Anyone who could pull off that easygoing playboy facade and kill people for cash in his spare time was impressive. I appeared to be what I was: an asshole. I didn't have his charm. I didn't fucking want it, either.

"Why you here, Colt?" I asked, tossing my keys onto the desk.

"Seems my next target is attached to someone around here. So I get to have a little Rosemary Beach fun while working. You seen the legs on some of these babes?"

I couldn't imagine why Benedetto would send him to Rosemary Beach. Unless it wasn't Benedetto. Lately, he was giving more and more power to the man he was grooming to take over: Cope. No one knew the guy's last name. We just knew he was in charge. And no one argued with him.

"Cope send you?" I asked.

"Yep. He's the only one I deal with now. DeCarlo doesn't call the shots much anymore. He leaves it up to Cope."

I suspected I was the only one Benedetto still dealt with personally. He was the closest thing I'd had to a father figure in my life. He'd grabbed me when I was a scared kid and given me a purpose.

"Don't piss him off," I warned Colt. I'd seen Cope kill just because he could. And that shit was scary. The dude didn't ask questions; he just finished the game and left. It was what someone like Benedetto had to do—but not me. I agreed to one thing only: I'd take them out if they deserved it. Not in the eyes of the law but in the eyes of me. That was all that mattered to me. If I thought I was saving someone who needed it, then I pulled the trigger.

Major chuckled. "Yeah, I got you. He's the king of badass."

He was more than that, but Major would figure that out soon enough.

"I've got work to do, Colt. You got a point to this?"

Major stood up and shrugged. "Naw, just wanted to say hi and I'm here for a while."

Great. Fantastic. Shit.

A knock on the door turned my attention away from Major. "Come in," I called out, hoping it wasn't more bullshit this early in the morning.

Those glasses caught my attention first. Her laughter from yesterday came back to me, and my stomach clenched. Had *she* been what made the nightmare come back? I fucking hoped not. I didn't want to fire her over this. But I couldn't work with her if she was going to raise my demons.

"Can I help you?" I asked, trying not to get flustered by the sight of her.

She glanced nervously at Major and then back to me. "My daughter's sick. She woke up with a fever this morning, and the caregiver I have for her is an elderly lady. I can't expect her to expose herself to whatever Franny has. I also need to take Franny to see a doctor."

Relief that I wouldn't have to see her today washed over me. "How long you think this'll take?"

Her entire body tensed up, and it was as if she was physically trying to restrain herself from snapping at me for my callous response. I almost grinned.

"Hopefully, I'll get a prescription from the doctor for her, and she'll be well enough for me to come in tomorrow," she said, in a tone that communicated exactly what her body was trying not to say. She was pissed at me.

"Kid doesn't have a father?" I replied, wanting to see her snap for some insane reason.

But instead of her getting defensive and smarting off at me, her face went pale. I heard Major mutter a curse word that I knew was meant for me. Fuck, was the kid's father dead or something? Damn my stupid mouth.

"I don't think so . . . no," she replied in a whisper, before stepping back and closing the door.

"You're a Grade A asshole," Major mumbled, sounding irritated. "She looks like a sweet thing. A very sexy sweet thing. And she's a single mom."

He was right, so I didn't argue. I owed her an apology.

Rose

Strep throat. This wasn't going to be better in twenty-four hours. I would need to stay home with Franny for two days, at the very least, before the antibiotics did their job well enough for me to return to work. However, letting my boss know that made me want to cringe.

River's—no, Captain's—words had been it for me. There was no reason for us to stay. I couldn't say this was a mistake. At least I knew what had become of the boy I had carried around in my heart for all these years. I wasn't depriving Franny of a good father. Captain was an asshole. She didn't need to know him. Besides, I wondered if he'd even believe me. I couldn't take that from him. This was enough.

I peeked into the bedroom we shared, and Franny was sleeping peacefully, thanks to the medicine they'd given her. I collected the cup of melted ice beside the bed, before tiptoeing back out of the room. Calling Captain was next on my list. If he gave me a hard time about it, then I'd just quit before he could fire me. There were other jobs to be had in this town. I could get one of them until we had enough money saved up to move yet again.

Taking care of us was what I did, and I was good at it. This

21

would not end in regret. This was simply a door that I could finally close so I could move on. The guilt I felt about dating other guys wouldn't haunt me any longer. I wouldn't see River's face smiling at me every time a guy asked me out. From now on, I would say yes if I liked the guy. I wouldn't live with self-blame and guilt another day.

I went outside to make the call so I wouldn't wake Franny. If I was lucky, I'd get Elle, and she'd handle it incorrectly. Then I could just quit. Easy.

"Hello?" Captain's deep voice vibrated over the phone. I hated the fact that I liked his stupid voice.

"Captain, this is Rose. My daughter has strep throat, and I'm going to need to stay with her for two days." I blurted it out quickly and then tensed, ready for his response.

"OK, yeah. Take however long you need," he replied.

I forgot to breathe a moment and stood there with my mouth hanging open. Had I heard the man correctly?

"And about my comment today," he said. "I'm sorry. It was rude and shitty. I shouldn't have asked you that. I respect the fact that you're a hardworking single mom."

Words I had been ready to shout at him all but evaporated as I stood in silent awe at what I was hearing.

"You there?" he asked. I managed to nod my head, although he couldn't see that.

Swallowing, I opened my mouth again and managed to squeak out, "Thank you."

Captain let out a heavy sigh and waited a moment.

Was he waiting for me to say more? He'd shocked me. I didn't know what to say.

"Just give me a call when you know you can come back in.

We'll manage without you while you take care of your daughter," he said, before ending the call. He didn't wait for me to say more, but I figured he had given up on me replying.

I held the phone in my hand and stared at it blankly. Had that really just happened?

"Mommy," Franny called from inside. I hurried back to her. I'd figure out Captain's motives later.

Fourteen years ago

"You like to eat, don't you?" he drawled, with an amused grin, from across the table.

If he wasn't so nice to look at, I'd ignore him, but I liked seeing him smile. Even if he was teasing me. My cheeks felt warm with embarrassment for inhaling my food so quickly. I never knew when food was going to stop coming. As long as full plates were set in front of me, I intended to enjoy them.

I just nodded my reply.

"They won't stop feeding you," he assured me, as if he'd read my mind.

This kid, who had been given this life, didn't know what it was like to be hungry. I did. I also knew that good things didn't last. You had to soak it up as it was happening.

"I kinda thought they might eat with us tonight, but Dad didn't come home in time for dinner. Mom's off pouting. This happens a lot. You'll get used to it."

I put another forkful of mashed potatoes into my mouth. As long as they fed me, I didn't care where they ate.

"You aren't a big talker."

I swallowed and put down my fork.

He was nice enough, although he liked teasing me. Maybe we could be friends while I stayed here, if I gave him a chance to get to know me.

"I like the chicken," I finally said, because I wasn't sure what else to say.

His face went from a grin to a full-blown smile, and he started laughing. My face burned this time, and he started shaking his head while he laughed. "No, that's"—he let loose another cackle of laughter—"that's good. I'm glad you like the chicken, Addison."

"It's Addy," I replied in a whisper.

He went silent and leaned in closer. "What did you say?"

I pushed my embarrassment away and met his gaze. "My name is Addy."

The corners of his mouth lifted, and the green of his eyes sparkled. "I like that. Addy."

"Thanks. Me, too. Addison's too long and sounds old."

His smile stayed in place, and he shrugged. "I don't think it sounds old, but Addy fits you."

"My mom called me Addy," I admitted, surprising myself. I'd never talked about her.

"What happened to your mom?"

I wanted to tell him. I never wanted to tell anyone, but I wanted to tell this boy. "She left me a long time ago . . . in a grocery-store parking lot . . ."

Captain

When my office door opened without a knock, I assumed it was Elle. She continued to confuse our having a sex life with her having some kind of power around here. "Knock next time," I snapped without looking up. She'd pout, and I wasn't in the mood.

"My hands were full with your coffee. I intercepted that tall, dark-haired girl you keep bringing around," Blaire replied.

I jerked my gaze up to see my sister standing in the doorway with a smirk and a cup of coffee.

"But I'm thinking with that attitude, I might keep this coffee for myself."

I had only met my sister a few years ago. I hadn't even known she existed until my biological father came and found me. But from the moment we met, she'd gone out of her way to make sure we became a family. And she'd succeeded. Blaire Finlay was hard to say no to.

"I'm sorry. I thought you were Elle," I explained.

Understanding lit her eyes, so similar to my own, as she walked over and set the cup on my desk. "In that case, I completely understand. She's annoying." Leave it to Blaire to be blunt. She always said what she was thinking.

"To what do I owe this pleasure?" I asked, taking my coffee and leaning back to study my sister, who was making herself comfortable in the chair across from my desk.

"Just missed you. I thought your moving to Rosemary Beach meant we would see each other more often, but you work all the time. I was complaining this morning, and Rush suggested I come see you and invite you over for dinner."

Rush Finlay was her husband and the son of the drummer of the world's most renowned rock band, Slacker Demon. They'd started releasing number one hits twenty years ago and were still at it. The world Rush came from was very different from Blaire's, but they worked together. He worshipped the ground she walked on and was a surprisingly great dad to their son.

"This place has consumed every last second. This is my first time actually starting up a restaurant, and it's more than I bargained for."

Blaire tilted her head, and her pale blond hair fell over one shoulder. "So is this a no to dinner?"

I was busy, but I knew if I told her no, she'd be sad, and I'd feel like shit. Then I'd get another visit today. From Rush. That visit wouldn't be friendly at all. I relented. "I'll be there. Tell me when."

She beamed at me, and I figured making her smile like that was worth finding the time to hang out with her family. "Great! How about tomorrow night?" she asked, clapping her hands together as if I'd just given her the best news ever.

"I can do tomorrow night."

"Perfect. Seven o'clock. And don't bring that girl. You can bring someone if you want, just not her. Or I can invite a friend or something . . ." She trailed off. I didn't know any of Blaire's friends who might be single, but I wasn't about to trust her not to try to set me up.

"I won't bring Elle, but I don't want you to invite anyone else, either. It'll just be a family thing."

Blaire smiled as she stood, and something about that smile made me nervous. Her mind was already spinning. Dammit. "I'll see you then," she said. "Don't overdo it. The place looks great, and I'm sure it'll be a success. Just take some time for yourself."

I nodded. In my entire life, only one other person had ever cared enough to give me these pointless little talks. I shoved the memory of her away. I was already dreaming about Addy again; I couldn't let her into my daily life, too.

"Got it," I assured her, just so she'd stop with the caring and leave. I didn't want her to care. Not when I was so raw emotionally.

"Tomorrow night, then," she repeated, as if I was going to forget. Then she left.

I took a long drink of my coffee and let it burn all the way down. There was paperwork to do and calls to make.

Moments after the door closed behind Blaire, someone knocked. Biting back a curse, I looked up. "Come in," I said, louder than necessary.

It slowly opened, and Rose's face peeked inside. "Sorry if I'm interrupting you. I just . . . I wanted to let you know I'm back and to thank you for understanding about Franny being sick. I'll work extra hours the rest of the week."

Being a detached hard-assed boss was easier when you didn't know the details of others' personal lives. But I knew now that Rose was a single mom, and that fucking changed things. She was so young, yet she had kept her kid and was raising her. I respected that.

Her large eyes blinked behind her glasses, and I wondered what she looked like without them. She was beautiful with them on, but I couldn't imagine how much more attractive she would be if she wasn't hiding behind them.

"Is she better now?" I asked, before I could stop myself.

Rose's tense expression eased, and she smiled, her face lighting up, and my gut clenched like it had when I'd heard her laughter the other day in the kitchen. Something about her smile struck a chord in me.

"Yes, thank you. She's much better and ready to get out and play again," Rose said, obvious love and relief in her voice. She loved her kid. There was no question about that.

"Good. I'm glad she's better. Don't worry about overtime. You can go back to regular working hours. I don't think we're that far behind."

She nodded. "OK. Do I need to find Elle to get my directions for the day?"

Elle would eat her up, so I shook my head no. Which was ridiculous, since Elle would soon be the head of the serving staff, and Rose would have to answer to her eventually. I couldn't protect her from Elle forever, and I shouldn't fucking have to, either. I'd have to fix that. Elle had no clue about Rose's life. She needed to ease up.

"Go back to the kitchen and help Brad. He's got another shipment in. At lunch today, the kitchen staff is going to prepare some of our signature dishes, and the serving staff will meet in the dining room for a tasting so you'll all know how to describe each dish to the customers."

"Yes, sir." She replied a little too quickly, as if she couldn't wait to get away from me, before she stepped back and closed the door, leaving me alone.

Rose

He hated my laugh, or maybe it was just the sound of my voice. Did he recognize it? Was that it? Did he hate the girl he thought had run off and left him? Was I a reminder of something he wanted to forget?

Stepping outside, I inhaled the warm breeze and took a moment to allow the pain in my chest to ease. Being near him was making the pain stronger. The things I had been able to push aside and the memories I had found a way to escape were now beating down my door. They'd begun slipping into my dreams; sometimes I couldn't breathe.

I wasn't sure what he thought had happened to me all those years ago. My choice had been swift, and I'd only had one thing in mind: protecting him. I'd caused enough trouble, and staying there would only have torn us apart in the end. She would have seen to that. She had left me with no other option. I had done what I needed to do.

It was obvious my laugh caused a reaction in him. His scrutinizing gaze locked onto me, and the coldness in his eyes robbed me of any enjoyment I was having. He could ruin my ability to smile with that look.

Brad had noticed it today at the tasting, too. I wasn't the

only one who saw River's strange behavior when I laughed. Brad had leaned in and whispered something about Elle barely tasting the food, and when I'd let out a small chuckle, River's eyes had zeroed in on me. Brad had looked annoyed and said, "What's his deal?" under his breath.

If he was recognizing my laugh, I needed to be more careful. I wasn't ready to come clean with him yet. He'd shown some kindness, and for a moment, I'd seen the boy I once knew under that cold exterior. But it wasn't enough for me to allow him into Franny's life.

Elle's glare whenever she looked my way reminded me of what I would not let into my daughter's life. If Elle was an example of the kind of woman River kept around in his life, he wasn't good enough for Franny. Simple fact was, I didn't trust him.

"You headed home?" Brad asked me just as I reached my car. I had been so lost in thought I hadn't heard him walk up behind me.

"Yeah, my daughter will be waiting for me," I said with a smile. I recognized the flirty attitude I was getting from him. I'd dealt with this from many men over the years. Sometimes I dated, but it never lasted, because men couldn't deal with the fact that Franny came first. I was a mother before all else.

"Would you and Franny be interested in joining me for pizza on the beach?"

His question surprised me, and I looked up from my search for the car keys in my purse. "What?" I asked, even though I'd heard him.

He grinned, and there was almost a dimple in his left cheek. His teeth were nice and white, too. He had a good smile. "I know I prepare gourmet meals as a profession, but I enjoy a good cheesy pizza as much as the next guy. There's a place I go to in Grayton Beach that's right on the water."

I stared up at him in shock. No one had ever asked me *and* Franny out. Most of the time, when guys found out about Franny, they made excuses and backed off. Brad, however, seemed completely cool with the fact that I had a nine-year-old daughter.

"Uh, well . . . yeah, sure. Franny loves pizza." I heard the surprise in my voice.

Brad chuckled again and nodded toward a white Ford truck. "I'll follow you home, and we can get Franny."

He seemed so pleased. I simply nodded again.

Brad was probably two years older than me, and he was tall, with dark hair and hazel eyes. He was built like someone who spent quality time at the gym. There were seven female servers in the restaurant who were young, single, and gorgeous. Why was he pursuing me? I knew two of those girls had a crush on him—they were always making up reasons to go to the kitchen to talk to him. He was polite and took it in stride, but he never encouraged them. Not that it stopped them from trying again. But I had assumed that meant he was attached. Maybe a girlfriend or a fiancée. It wasn't my business, so I didn't ask.

"I'll see you in a few," he said now with a wink, then turned to head over to his truck.

OK, so maybe this was a friend kind of thing. I mean, he invited Franny without blinking an eye. And we had enjoyed each other's company the few days that River had put us together in preparation for the grand opening.

Finally, my fingers landed on the key ring at the bottom of my purse. I had unlocked the door and started to get in when I saw something in the corner of my eye. Glancing back, I saw that River was walking out the door with Elle. She had her arms wrapped around his waist, and his hand rested on her hip. I could see her laughing up at him.

That wasn't my River. The more I was around him, the more my heart mourned the boy I'd loved. Something had turned him into this man. A beautiful, detached, hard man. I didn't want my mood to plummet. I drove away without looking back once.

Thirteen years ago

"Where's Addy?" River asked his mother. I could hear him from the closet I was locked in. It was dark, and I really had to use the bathroom, but I knew not to knock or make a sound. She'd leave me in here longer.

"Addison is being punished. Go wash up for dinner. Daddy will be here tonight. He called and promised to be home. We can have a family meal." Her overexcited voice made me cringe. I was terrified of that voice.

"Why is Addy being punished? Where is she, Mom?" River sounded angry.

His mother sighed loudly. "That is not your business. You go wash up like a good boy."

"I'm thirteen years old. Don't talk to me like I'm five. I'm grown-up, Mom. Now, tell me where you put Addy. Now!" He roared the last bit, and I squeezed my eyes tight, praying she wouldn't hit him. He wouldn't hit her back. He never did. He just let her hit him until

she was over it. Then she would run off to her room, and he would find me.

"Her name is Addison. Addy sounds ridiculous. And do not yell at me," she said, still sounding way too happy. "Your father will be here any minute. Let's not fight. With her out of the way, we can enjoy our meal."

I heard a loud crash, and I jumped back against the wall. "If you don't tell me where she is, I'm going to throw every damn dish in this kitchen against the wall." River's voice sounded so much older than a thirteen-year-old boy's.

"Please, God, don't let her hit him," I whispered, wondering if God would listen if I prayed for someone else. I knew praying for myself didn't work; I'd tried that.

A loud, high-pitched squeal made my heart clench. "Let go of my arm!"

"No. I'm not letting you hit me, and I'm not letting you lock her up. Where. Is. She."

"Please, please, please, God," I begged quietly in the dark. He was pushing her too far.

"Ow!" she screamed. "You're hurting my wrist."

"Then tell me where Addy is!"

"In the hall closet." She let out in an angry growl. "But if you go after her, I'll lock you in the attic."

"Noooo!" I cried under my breath. The attic was so hot and dirty. Every time she locked me up in there, I had nightmares for days afterward.

"You aren't putting me anywhere. I'll tell Dad," he said. Then his footsteps drew closer toward me.

I wished he'd just leave me in here. We would both pay for this later. She'd do something terrible.

The doorknob turned, and I squinted against the light as I looked up at him. He was so tall, and at that moment, with that fierce expression on his face, I was sure he was my angel. Maybe God had heard me and sent me River.

He dropped to his knees and held out a hand to me. "It's OK, Addy. I'm here." His voice was gentle. Nothing like what I'd heard him use with his mother.

"If you take her out of that closet, I will call social services and have her sent away. I don't have to keep her here. She's not what I wanted. She's a mean child."

I didn't want to go to a group home, and I didn't want to lose River, but I kept my mouth closed. Among my options, there were two kinds of evil. I knew this one; I didn't know the one I would face out there. I also wouldn't have River to stand up for me.

"If you send her away, I'll tell Dad you're taking pills again," River said, turning to look at her. "I know. I have proof. I'll tell him, and he'll leave this time. For good."

I wasn't sure what pills he was talking about, but her face paled. She didn't say anything but turned and stalked away.

"Come on, Addy. She'll lock herself away for the night now. I beat her at her own game," he said, taking my hand in his and giving it a gentle squeeze. "Let's get you some food."

"Your dad is coming home," I whispered, afraid she'd hear me and come back.

He scowled and shook his head. "No, he's not. He's with his secretary. Come on, let's go eat."

Captain

It was her laugh. Brad had fucking made her laugh enough today that I'd had plenty of opportunities to evaluate it. Telling myself that Rose's laugh reminded me of *hers* was an understatement. Rose *had* Addy's laugh. Even the way her eyes danced and the way she tilted her head were identical to Addy's. It was hard to watch and listen to.

I'd had to bite back a snarled demand that she stop laughing twice today. I hated how the sound of it made me feel, because with its warmth came the sharp pain of loss. Something I thought I'd overcome years ago. I'd have to keep Rose at a distance. She was a hard worker and a single mom. I couldn't fire her. I just had to avoid her, or I was going to crack. Emotional damage came with those memories. Even after all these years, it was a trauma I'd never forget. My actions following Addy's death had changed me. I'd never be the same person again.

With each man I killed, I lost a little more of my soul. Even if those men deserved death, being the one to end their lives took a piece of me. I knew I'd never love again, because I couldn't. My emotions weren't normal; I was both haunted by them and cut off from them in a way that couldn't be healed.

When I pulled my truck up to the marina where I kept my boat, I saw Elle's car. I'd told her I wasn't in the mood for company tonight, but she hadn't listened. She rarely did. Maybe what I needed was to let her take my mind off the past.

I'd lived on the boat for most of my adult life. It moved with me, and having it meant I could leave at any time. I liked the freedom it gave me. I had missed it when I was in Texas, my most recent state of residence. Houses brought back bad memories for me. I couldn't bring myself to stay in a house.

My boat gave me peace.

Stepping inside, I noticed Elle in the small kitchen, fixing sandwiches. When she did stuff like this, I felt guilty for leading her on, if that was what I was doing. She had her issues, but she wasn't all that bad. When I needed stress relief, she was there. I just didn't have what she needed emotionally. I wasn't ever going to want more. I'd never care about her deeply, let alone love her.

Her long brown hair swung over her shoulder as she glanced back at me. Then she smiled. That smile was safe. It didn't cause painful constrictions in my chest. She didn't remind me of all I'd lost. She could laugh, and it wouldn't affect me. Yet another reason I liked Elle.

"I know you said you weren't in the mood for company, but I figured you needed to eat, and I was hungry, so I fixed us some sandwiches. We can eat together, at least. Then I'll leave."

She knew she wasn't leaving as well as I did. But I just nodded and walked over to the fridge to grab a beer. "You want something?" I asked.

"A beer is good," she replied, a little too happily. She knew she'd won. I was too tired to care.

I took two beers and put hers on the counter before picking up my sandwich. It was the bigger of the two. She rarely ate large portions. I doubted she'd eat half of the sandwich she'd fixed for herself.

Taking a bite, I leaned back and watched the black waves outside. It was calm tonight. No wind to make things rough.

"You don't want to sit?" she asked, breaking into my thoughts.

I shook my head and took another bite.

"You seem tense today. Like you're ready to explode at any moment."

She watched me too closely. If she connected my mood to Rose, things would get ugly. Yet another reason to distance myself from Rose.

You're protecting her. Just like Addy.

The thought was there before I could push it away. It was the truth, of course. I was protecting Rose. Simply because her laugh reminded me of Addy. I could lie to myself and say I was intrigued by her because she was a single mom and a hard worker. But that wasn't it. I knew it wasn't.

"Closer we get to the opening, the more tense I get. Gonna have to deal with it," I replied without emotion.

I could see Elle playing with her sandwich instead of eating it. She wanted more from me. I'd known the day would come when she would push for more. It always did. And I always sent them on their way. More wasn't me.

"I wish you'd open up to me. I'm here to listen to you. I care about you. I thought we were getting closer. Just yesterday, in your office . . ."

"We fucked, Elle. That's all it was. A fuck. I told you in the beginning, I just fuck, babe. You want closer, you're with the wrong guy."

My words were cold, but that was me. She needed to hear it.

"You're not the hard, untouchable guy you want me to believe you are. I've seen you let your guard down. So is it just me? Is that it? You don't want me?"

This was the moment. I could hurt her and lie, say yes, and send her on her way. But she was my head server. I didn't love her, but I wasn't going to be cruel, either.

"It's not you," I bit out. I wasn't going to share a piece of myself or my past. However, she needed to understand that I was not the guy she was looking for. "Gave my heart away a long time ago."

I heard her quick intake of breath. She hadn't been expecting that.

Taking another bite of my sandwich, I reached for my beer and shoved off from the counter. I needed distance from Elle. From everyone.

"Are you saying you're in love with someone else?"

It was more than that, but I just gave a nod and drank my beer.

"Who? Where is she?" Elle asked, her voice rising just enough to let me know she was pissed.

"Not talking about it."

"You're not talking about it?" she all but screamed behind me. "We've been fucking, as you call it, for weeks, and you left out the fact that you were in love with someone else? What are we doing, then? Huh?"

"Fucking," I replied.

"You're a . . . you're a . . . ugh! I can't believe I—" She

stopped and let out a growl, then headed for the door. "I won't be used," she said, just as she was about to leave.

"Good," was my only response. She shouldn't allow herself to be used.

"That's all you're going to say? Seriously?"

I set my beer down and finally turned to look at her. The fury on her face was what I expected. This was the way it always ended. Even though I warned them in the beginning that I'd never want more. "Did I tell you from the start that there would ever be more than fucking from me?"

She glared at me but finally nodded.

"Correct. I didn't. You were the one who wanted to change the rules."

I could see the pain in her eyes, and I felt guilty for putting it there. I felt guilty every damn time.

Elle didn't say more. She turned and left.

Finally, I was alone.

Rose

Franny was curled up on the sofa asleep when I got home. Mrs. Baylor was sitting in the recliner with a book in her lap. She smiled up from what she was reading to greet me with a whisper.

"I tried to persuade her to go to bed, but she wanted to wait up for you. She played hard today. We even made three dozen macadamia nut cookies. You need to take most of those to work with you tomorrow; we won't be able to eat them all."

Brad's truck pulled up behind mine in the driveway, and I glanced back toward him. I hadn't expected Franny to be asleep so early. Typically, she was a night owl. But I also wasn't about to ask Mrs. Baylor to stay and watch her while I went out for pizza with a man.

"Thank you for today. I know she had fun," I said, as I gazed at my daughter. She was my world. I would never be able to thank Mrs. Baylor enough for being so good to her.

Mrs. Baylor stood up and cleared her throat softly. "Well, it looks like you have company." Her voice held an amused tone.

I turned back to see Brad stepping out of his truck. He looked uncertain about whether he should proceed.

"He's a friend from work. I'll just go explain that Franny is asleep and send him on his way."

"Nonsense. You need to make some friends, and from where I'm standing, that friend is a fine sight."

My face flushed red. "Franny waited up for me. I want to be here if she wakes up."

"And you can be. But that doesn't mean you can't fix that young man a glass of wine and invite him to sit on your lovely porch. The stars are beautiful tonight."

I doubted Brad drank wine. He seemed more like a beer drinker. And he was hungry. All I had was leftover chicken pot pie from the night before. I did have the makings for a pizza, though. Franny and I had pizza night once a week, so I always kept the kitchen stocked with what we needed.

Mrs. Baylor patted my arm as she walked past me. "You'll figure it out." Then she smiled over at Brad before walking across the yard and toward her house.

I wasn't sure if I should even bring up making a pizza here. He seemed really excited about the place in Grayton Beach. Asking a guy over for dinner wasn't something I'd ever done. And although he was becoming a friend, I was still nervous.

"Everything OK?" he asked, as he walked toward me. His brow was creased in a concerned frown.

"Yeah, it's just that Franny fell asleep. She was sick earlier this week, and she's still not a hundred percent yet." I paused instead of offering to make him pizza. Brad was nice enough to accept even if he didn't want to.

"That's understandable," he replied, then glanced over my shoulder at the house before looking back at me. "Would you be up for ordering pizza instead?"

That was the reassurance I needed. "I actually have everything we need to make pizza here. I could cook for you," I offered.

A smile spread across his lips. "I'd like that."

"OK, let me wake Franny and move her to her bed. She'll want to talk to me for a few minutes, I imagine. Come on in-side. I don't have any beer, but I do have sweet tea," I told him, feeling a silly smile on my face that I couldn't help. This was nice. He was nice.

"I'm a big fan of sweet tea," he replied.

I wasn't good at this, but he didn't seem to mind. I led the way inside, then quickly made him a glass of tea. Franny slept through it all. I didn't want her waking up and being confused by a strange man in the house. She wasn't used to men being in our home at all.

"Here you go," I said with a smile, as I handed Brad the glass. "Just give me a second to move Franny." I really wanted to ask him to step outside while I did it, but that would seem rude.

"I'll just enjoy the view of the water from your back porch," he said with a wink, before heading for the door.

It was like he could read my mind. I almost said thank you but stopped myself. When he was safely outside, I went over to the sofa and gently ran my hand over Franny's hair. "You need to get into bed," I whispered close to her ear.

She stirred before slowly blinking her eyes as she tried to focus on me. "M'kay," she mumbled, then snuggled deeper into the sofa.

"I can't carry you, so you're going to have to stand up. I'll walk you to bed."

"M'kay," she said again, and held up an arm for me to take. Grinning, I helped her stand and tucked her close to my side.

"I love you," I told her.

"Love you, too," she replied in a groggy voice.

I wanted to give her everything. All the things I never had. And for the most part, I'd done that. I had given her a stable life, and she had no doubt that she was safe and loved.

When we got to the bedroom, she went directly to the bed and curled up without opening her eyes again. I took the covers and tucked her in, then pressed a kiss to her head.

"Do you like him?" she whispered, opening her eyes to look at me.

"Who?" I asked, wondering if she was dreaming. She often talked in her sleep.

"The guy on the back porch."

"Oh!" I replied, surprised.

She smiled, then closed her eyes again, pulling the covers up to her chin. "Save me some pizza for tomorrow."

With a laugh, I kissed her one more time before going to join Brad outside on the porch.

Captain

Twelve years ago

I waited outside the school for Addy. Every day, she'd meet me out here, and we would walk home together. Once we had ridden the bus, but when I'd punched a kid in the noise for shoving Addy out of his way and knocking her to the floor, I'd been suspended from bus privileges. Which was fine with us. We enjoyed the walk home.

Addy always told me about her day, and I loved hearing her talk. She'd laugh at things I said, and I'd try my hardest to be funny. It felt like those laughs belonged to me. Addy didn't laugh enough at home. My mother made sure of that. But every chance I got, I gave her a reason to laugh. It gave me more pleasure than anything else.

The doors opened, and Addy stepped outside. Her blond curls hung down her back, and she squinted into the sunlight as she looked for me. Stepping forward, I waved my hand, and just like that, her face lit up. Again, that smile belonged to me. She only gave it to me. My chest got tight every time.

"Hey, River, are we still on for Friday night? My parents are out of town, so you could come over and watch a movie." It was Mallory

Buchanan, who came up beside me and flipped her hair over her shoulder dramatically.

"Yeah, sure," I agreed.

Mallory had been flirting with me for two weeks, so I'd asked her out for Friday. I didn't usually flirt with girls or talk to them in front of Addy. I could see it made her uncomfortable whenever I did. I glanced back at Addy and saw that her smile was gone and she was walking more slowly. She wasn't in a hurry to get to me now. Why did Mallory have to talk to me out here?

"Yeah, I gotta go," I said to Mallory, without taking my gaze off Addy.

I hurried toward her. The forced smile on my face was meant to ease her mind. Addy had become my best friend. She understood me in a way no one else did, and I got her, too. We looked out for each other and told each other everything. Except that I tried not to bring up girls in front of her.

"Hey, you," I said, when I got close enough.

"Hey," she replied, and her cheeks turned a light shade of pink. "I didn't mean to interrupt you."

She always did this, always acted like she was in my way. I knew enough to be careful around her, but I hated that she thought she wasn't more important than those other girls. She was the most important person in my life. She always would be.

"Don't be silly. You're my favorite girl. You know that," I said, and put my arm around her shoulders to pull her in for a quick hug. "How about when we get home, we go out to the pond and do our homework there?" She loved the pond. We had to walk along a path through the woods behind our house to get to it, but she loved going.

The smile I'd been looking for was back as she nodded her head. "I'd like that."

I'd dreamed about her again. But this time, there was no blood. It had just been us. The way we were. The easy way I felt around her. Seeing her smile at me and feeling complete with her.

Standing out on the bow of my boat with a cup of coffee, I watched the sun rise while memories of Addy came back to me. It wasn't that I'd forgotten those moments. I remembered everything about her. Every single moment we'd had was forever etched in my brain. It had just been so long since I'd given in and thought of them.

The sharp pain in my chest was tucked in so tight I wouldn't be able to shake it loose. It came with the memories. It was why I tried not to remember. But as I stood here on the water, watching the beauty of the morning sun slowly lightening the sky, it felt right. Addy loved water, and she loved to watch the sun rise. We'd watched so many sunrises together. She would have adored living on a boat. It would have been an adventure. As long as she'd been with me, she'd been up for anything.

I heard footsteps coming up behind me. I knew from the heaviness of the footfalls that it was a man. Someone with purpose. I didn't need to turn around. Listening was more important than seeing in my line of work.

"Cope," I said, then took another drink of my coffee while the sun blazed bright over the water.

"Cap," he replied. Both of our names had been shortened by DeCarlo. His was Copeland, but everyone called him Cope.

"I don't work for DeCarlo anymore. Can't see why you'd be here." I never doubted that DeCarlo would try to pull me back in. He hadn't wanted me out. But the small sliver of my soul that I'd been able to hold on to was the piece that only Addy's memories kept alive. I hadn't been willing to lose that.

"Came to warn you," he said, in what always reminded me of a growl. He was the angriest human I'd ever met. Combine that with his massive frame, and he could be intimidating. He was a solid brick wall covered in tats. "Someone's here. Don't know who, but they traced you here."

I frowned. "Someone after me because of a former job?"

He shrugged. "Don't know. You've just been tracked down. Keep your eyes open."

Shit. I didn't want to bring my former hell anywhere near my sister and her family. "How long they been here?"

"At least a month. Maybe more."

And they still hadn't done anything? That wasn't typical. This was screwy. "I'll find them."

"I've got to fix some of Major's shit," Cope said, then headed back down the dock. He wasn't a man of many words, but I'd always liked him.

I wasn't worried about someone tracking me. If they were here, they wouldn't sneak up on me; I'd feel their presence first. Only a matter of time before I figured out who it was.

Rose

I had touched up my roots last night after Brad left, so my hair was an even darker red today. Coloring my blond hair wasn't something I had wanted to do. It was high-maintenance, but it was part of my cover. That and the glasses made me look different enough from the girl he once knew. I had also grown up, and my cheekbones were more defined, my breasts had filled out, and my hips had a flare to them after giving birth that they hadn't had before. I'd also lost that twinkle of wonder in my eyes.

On that first day, I'd believed deep down that he'd recognize me anyway. That he would know who I was, that my facade would be in vain, because he'd be a wonderful man who knew me instinctively and would adore our daughter once I told him about her. But that hadn't happened. He'd hardly even glanced at me. The most he'd ever spoken to me was to tell me what I needed to do.

Last night, when Brad and I had our pizza date, I'd realized that I missed having that kind of connection. I hadn't experienced it in my adult life. Someone to laugh with and talk to about adult stuff. I wasn't saying I could fall in love with Brad, because honestly, I didn't think there was even a slight chance.

As much as I didn't want to admit it, River still held a large piece of my heart that Captain hadn't been able to kill.

Sometimes, when he wasn't looking at me, I could see his thoughtful expression as he worked something out in his head, and I'd feel like I was in the presence of River in that moment. Those little glimpses were enough to keep a firm hold on my heart. But loving River had been my world. You can't tell your heart to stop loving someone. I'd been trying that for years, simply to ease the ache of losing him.

Taking a deep breath, I walked into the dining room ready to face another day. I expected to see Elle ordering everyone around, but instead there was River—Captain—shouting out commands and complaining about things that had been done wrong. I quickly hurried over to listen to him before clocking in and putting away my purse.

"The flatware has to be rolled to the specifications given. Elle gave three classes on this, and all of you needed to attend at least one. The flatware rolling will be done by every server every night at close until there are three hundred prepared and ready to go. This shit isn't anywhere near right. Can one of you demonstrate how this should be done?"

No one raised their hand. The strained look on Captain's face had silenced them all. Stepping forward, I held my hand up. "I can." I'd been through two of Elle's classes, and she'd taken every opportunity to make an example of me. I had wrapped more than thirty sets all by myself one day, because she kept saying my work was sloppy. I had no doubt I could do it.

Captain's eyes locked on me, and he picked up a linen napkin and a set of flatware. "Show me."

I didn't let his piercing eyes intimidate me, but I also didn't hold his gaze. There was always the chance that he'd finally see the eyes behind the glasses. I took the supplies and placed them on the table he was standing beside. Then I wrapped them up more perfectly than anything Elle had ever done.

"Looks like someone paid attention." The relief was obvious in his voice. "Elle is out for the next few days. I need you to teach this bunch how to do this," he said in a soft tone, then lifted his gaze to everyone else. "If you can't wrap the fucking flatware properly in two days' time, you're fired. Is that understood?"

The tension in the room was heavy, but they all replied in the affirmative. That meant I had the rest of the day to teach them the proper way to wrap flatware.

"Good job," Captain said, in a voice that stirred memories. There was kindness in his tone. Almost as if he felt we were a team. We had been the best team once.

"Thanks," I replied.

"If any of them give you a hard time, let me know. I'm not opening this place with any slackers on board. There's a pile of applications on my desk from people who would gladly take their places."

I didn't doubt that. Other than the Kerrington Country Club, this was the only place in town that would bring in big tips.

"OK," I said, looking away from him and back down at my hands.

"Get to it," he barked at the rest of the room, causing me to jump. Then he patted my shoulder and walked out of the dining room.

The grumbles and complaints started as whispers and grew louder quickly. I thought I caught Elle's name a few times. No one seemed concerned with doing what he'd just ordered them to do.

"Hey, Rose, you good?" Brad asked, as he stepped into the dining room from the kitchen.

I held up a napkin in my hand and forced a smile. "I have to teach everyone how to roll flatware," I explained.

He looked around at the others, noticing their lack of concern, then frowned. "Hey!" he called out, getting their attention. When all eyes were on him, he pointed to me. "Y'all need to learn how to roll the fucking flatware, and Rose doesn't have all damn day. Pay attention."

Several of the females smiled at Brad as if they'd do whatever he wanted them to do. He was single and attractive, so I didn't blame them. They stopped gossiping about where Elle might be and listened as I started the first of many lessons that day.

The word was that Captain had broken things off with Elle, and she was at home, pouting. Whatever the case, I was relieved to have a break from her for the next few days. But it was too much to hope that she wouldn't come back. Girls like her didn't give up without a fight.

Once everyone was clued in about why Elle wasn't at work, they seemed more willing to listen to the flatware lesson. Brad checked in on me every thirty minutes or so to be sure I had their attention. I liked that about him. He was helpful and seemed to care. Again, it was a nice feeling. One I hadn't had in a very long time.

"Hey," Brad said now. "I tried a new entrée today for the menu. You interested in helping me taste it? We could eat it here or go back to your place and share it with Franny. A kid's opinion might be good."

I lifted my eyes to meet his while I polished the tables. I hadn't heard him come in, but there he was again, being nice. "Uh, yeah. That sounds good. I mean, going to my place. Franny will need dinner."

A grin broke across his face, making him appear even more handsome. "Great. I'll pack everything up and meet you back here in a few." He hurried back to the kitchen.

With a pleased smile on my lips, I bent down to finish polishing the thick mahogany wood of the tabletop I was working on. Captain had said they needed to shine.

"You and Brad seeing each other?" Captain's deep voice filled the room, making my heart flutter. Frustrated, I shoved the feeling away and stood up to look at him. His expression wasn't friendly or curious but, rather, stern.

"We're, uh, friends. I think," I replied. Because honestly, I wasn't sure what we were yet.

"You think?" He seemed annoyed by my answer.

Straightening my spine, I held his gaze and gave him back the same annoyed expression he was giving me. "I don't see how this is your business."

A smirk touched his lips, and he tilted his head slightly to the left, but his eyes were hard. Nothing like River's. Not when he looked like that. "Brad's the best chef in the Southeast. I won't fire him. It'll be you that's gone if things don't work out. Understood?"

The ache in my chest was back. I hated seeing this side of

him. It was something I'd never experienced directed at me. Letting go of the past was hard, but he was making it easier with moments like these. I'd never be able to say goodbye to River—he'd always be a part of me—but I was preparing myself to let go of him.

"I understand," I replied through clenched teeth.

"Hey, Rose . . ." Brad's voice trailed off as he walked into the room. "Oh, hey, Captain. I tried out that entrée we discussed. Rose and I are going to her place to test it." He held up the carryout boxes in his hands. "We'll let you know our verdict."

Captain gave a stiff nod and left the room without a word.

Captain

I was in a shitty mood. Eating dinner with my sister wasn't something I wanted to do tonight, but canceling on her wasn't an option, either. If I tried to back out of it, she'd pout, and her husband would show up at my house pissed. So to avoid the drama, I decided to go.

Pulling up outside their mansion on the beach, I did a quick scan of the cars in the driveway and was relieved to see that it was just us. She hadn't invited the rest of her friends. Tonight I wasn't in the mood for all the happy couples and their kids.

When I reached the door, I rang the bell and waited. I could hear small feet running inside just before a *thump* hit the door.

"I got it!" my nephew called out. He was three going on twenty.

The door swung open, and I looked down to see Nate Finlay smiling up at me with a big, toothy grin. His silver-gray eyes were his father's. Heck, most of the kid was like his father. Blaire couldn't claim much.

"Hey, Unca Cap," he said, as he held out his fist for me to bump.

I reached down and bumped his fist, then made sure to

"blow it up," or he'd make me do it again until I got it right. I'd learned that lesson already. "Hey, kid," I said.

"We're eatin' mash 'tatoes," he announced, as if that was the best thing in the world.

"That's the only item on the menu he cares about," Blaire said, walking up behind him. "I promise I made more than just mashed potatoes."

The smells coming from the kitchen made me hungry. I was ready for some food. What Brad had cooked at the restaurant had smelled incredible, but then he'd used that meal to impress Rose.

Thinking about that pissed me off more. I didn't want to admit to myself that I didn't like the idea of Rose with Brad, but fuck if that wasn't true. Thinking about Addy had screwed with my head. It was making me blur the line with Rose. Hell, I'd barely had a conversation with Rose. I had no claim on her other than that she reminded me of Addy. She brought back memories I'd tried hard to repress.

Telling her I'd fire her had been cold and uncalled for, but deep down, I wanted to do just that. I wanted an excuse to get her away from me. She was possibly the best worker I had, but I was trying to run her off because of my haunted past. It wasn't fair to her, and once again, I owed her an apology. This shit didn't need to become a pattern.

"What's with the frown? Mashed potatoes aren't that bad," Blaire said, studying me closely.

Blaire knew nothing of my past, and I wanted to keep it that way. "I love mashed potatoes. I've just had a long day. A lot on my mind, with the restaurant opening in a week."

My sister did not look convinced.

"Ribs are ready," Rush called from the kitchen.

Blaire grinned again. "I cooked the sides. I put him on the grill."

Ribs sounded good. "I'm starved."

"Perfect. Let's feed you."

"Mash 'tatoes!" Nate cheered as he ran ahead of us.

The kid had no idea how good his life was. His dad adored him, and his mother loved him unconditionally. His world was so much different from the one I'd lived in. Blaire's life had started out good, but after her twin sister was killed in a car accident, it had all gone to hell. I was glad she'd gotten a second chance. She deserved it.

Blaire had the life I had wanted for Addy. The one we used to sit and dream about together. Addy would have been an incredible mother. She had a heart so goddamn big it overpowered any evil we had to walk through. If I hadn't needed her so much, I could have saved her. Gotten her out sooner. But I'd wanted her close to me.

Eleven years ago

I didn't even go inside when I got home from my date. I knew Addy wouldn't be inside. Mom was at her newest fund-raiser event tonight. It was the only reason I had agreed to go anywhere without Addy. I knew she'd be safe.

I still hadn't been able to enjoy myself or the girl, who had quickly gotten naked for me. My thoughts had been with Addy and how I needed to check on her. Thinking of her alone bothered me. She shouldn't be alone. I didn't need sex, anyway. I could get that during school hours if I needed to.

I walked around to the back of the house and headed out to the path I knew would lead me to Addy's favorite spot by the pond. I could see her blond hair in the moonlight before I could see anything else. I loved her hair.

I stepped on a limb and gave my presence away. She jerked, turning around to see me approaching her. The look of fear on her face quickly faded into a pleased smile. The one only I got. I'd watched her smile at other guys. No one got this smile but me. The smile that made her eyes light up and sparkle. If another guy ever did get that smile, I wasn't sure I could handle it. I'd hurt someone.

"You're back," she said. The happy tone in her voice felt like warm butter.

"Yeah, wasn't much fun."

She smirked, then glanced away from me, back toward the water. "What, she didn't put out quick enough?" There was a bitterness to her tone that I didn't like.

"Uh, no, that wasn't it. I would just rather be here."

Addy turned her head toward me slowly, and her eyes looked like they were searching my face for any sign of a lie. "Really?"

"Yeah, really. I'd always rather be with you."

She chewed her bottom lip a moment, and then a frown puckered her brow. "Then why did you go?"

I wasn't sure. Because I knew I'd get laid? Because . . . hell, I didn't know. I would rather be with Addy. I'd always rather be with Addy, but lately, when I looked at her, I thought things. Things I needed to stop thinking. She was my best friend, and she needed me as much as I needed her. We fought a daily battle in that house, and we relied on each other to get through it all.

It was just that when I let myself go, I imagined how it would taste to kiss her lips, how soft her skin would feel. What kinds of sounds she'd make when I touched her under her shirt or slipped my hands down into her panties.

Fuck, I couldn't think about that. I looked away from her, out at the water. Addy was special. She was perfect and mine to protect. Even from me. "I went because I had guy needs, that's all. I'm here now. Where I want to be," I finally answered her.

She didn't reply, and I didn't look at her, for fear that my thoughts would go the way I fought hard to keep them from veering.

"You want to go inside and make some popcorn before she gets home?" Addy asked, with a smile in her voice.

My answer had been enough for her. She wasn't going to press for more. She never did. I turned to look back at her, and I knew then, without a doubt, that she was my center. She was my home. That house, run by parents who were too fucked-up to know the difference, wasn't home for me. Addy was. She always would be. One day, I'd give her a mansion, and we'd have kids. She'd live like a princess.

"Yeah, let's go sneak some popcorn," I replied, standing up and reaching my hand out to her. She slipped hers into mine, and I squeezed it tightly.

The smile on her face was better than any popcorn could ever be.

Rose

It was finally the night of the restaurant's grand opening, and the place was booked solid. For the last week, we had all worked until midnight every night, getting the place ready for the big event. Brad hadn't come over again, but he had made sure to sneak me things he was trying out for the menu during my break. He even sent me home with a gourmet grilled cheese sandwich and homemade potato chips for Franny a couple of nights. She'd charmed him, which wasn't surprising. She had that effect on people.

Captain had avoided me. Between all the work and staying away from me and keeping his distance from Elle, he had to be exhausted. Elle had returned, determined to act as if she was fine. We all got to hear about her dates, because she told the girls who cared so loudly that everyone else got all the details, too. If she was hoping to make Captain jealous, she was failing. He was ignoring her.

I almost felt sorry for her. Almost.

"You think Elle would kill me if I tried to make a move on Captain?" one of the other servers, Patricia, asked me, as she cut her eyes over my shoulder and gave a saucy grin in his direction. I glanced back over my shoulder to see Captain surveying the room while he talked to Brad.

"Probably, but do you really want to date the boss? Look at where that left Elle," I said honestly. It took a strong-minded female to come back after being shaken off by the man in charge, and everyone knew it.

Patricia pouted, and her very pink painted lips looked even bigger than usual. "The only other hottie here is Brad, and everyone knows he has a thing for you." She turned her attention back to me. "You do like him, right?"

Did I like him? Yes, I did, but we were friends. He was flirty at times, but mostly we just talked and laughed. "Um, well, he's a nice guy. I like spending time with him, but we aren't in a relationship or anything. We're just friends."

Her dark brown eyes lit up, and she batted her lashes before turning back to the two men. This time, her eyes were locked on Brad. "Great. Thanks!" she said, before heading toward them with a sway to her hips and a determined gleam in her eyes.

I could have stood there and watched, or I could have finished setting the tables and lighting the candles. I chose the latter and got to work. If Brad was interested in her, then good for him. It wouldn't hurt my friendship with him. At least, I didn't think it would.

We were each given three tables to cover. Captain wanted to make sure every guest was given the most attention possible. I had two four-tops and a two-top, so I wasn't overloaded, but the pressure was on to be perfect.

Brad was getting high praise from the diners, and everyone was enjoying the food. It went pretty smoothly, considering it was opening night.

I glanced around to see Captain talking to an older, obviously wealthy and important man who had a beautiful younger woman at his side. I'd have guessed it was his daughter if his hand wasn't settled on her waist possessively.

The man was smiling and seemed pleased to be chatting with Captain.

"That's Arthur Stout," Patricia said, whispering beside me. "The owner of this place."

Well, then, that made sense. I nodded and headed into the kitchen. Table seven's order was nearly up.

I walked back to the serving line and saw Brad organizing orders and laying out steaming plates. He had a bandanna tied around his head to hold back his shaggy hair. He looked up and shot me a grin.

"Hey," he said, before focusing on the dish he was plating.

"Seven is up," Henry, one of the other cooks, called out to me.

"Great. Thanks," I replied, turning to one of the food servers waiting to the side. "Take it to seven. Left to right. I'll follow behind."

One of the things Captain insisted on was that the main server of the table shouldn't bring the food. They were to follow behind, ready to address anything that was wrong or get the guests anything they requested.

I had turned to leave when Brad called out, "Hey, friend."

Unsure if that greeting was meant for me, I stopped and looked back at him.

He winked and shook his head. "I need to step up my game." Then he went back to work, still grinning.

Was he talking about what I had said to Patricia? Had she told him?

"Flirt on your own time. You have people to serve, and he has food to cook. No distractions, Rose." Captain's hard voice startled me, and I jerked my gaze up to see him glowering at me from the doorway of the kitchen.

I'd been working to be beyond good tonight, but to be excellent and get this treatment from him? *I haven't been flirting, thank you very much—I've been working!* Why wasn't he correcting Brad? Biting my tongue, I met his angry glare with one of my own before walking out past him without a word.

"Rose," Captain called out, in a clipped voice.

I wanted to keep walking and ignore him, but I'd draw attention from the others in the hallway who were watching us. I sucked it up and stopped to look back at my boss. "Yes, sir?" I bit out.

His eyes flared a moment, and I wondered what I'd done to make him so pissed. "Acknowledge me when I give you instructions." His voice was low, and the warning tone in it only made me angrier.

"You should direct your instructions to those who need them. I did nothing wrong." I tried to keep the acid out of my voice, but it was difficult.

"Told you Brad is the best. Don't want his head anywhere but on the food."

"I'm not distracting him. I was getting my table's food sent out," I shot back in defense.

"Then why was his focus on you when he should have

been busting his ass on the shit in front of him? Don't play dumb with me, Rose. I know women, sugar. I know them too damn well."

That was it. Captain had pushed me too far. "I'll finish the evening, and then I'm gone. That's what you want, after all. I'm not going to work here just to be accused of stuff I didn't do." I was louder than I should have been, but I didn't care. I spun on my heel and stalked away from the infuriating man I'd made the mistake of uprooting my life for.

Captain

Shit. I stood staring at Rose as she walked through the door and into the dining room. She was right. It was *Brad* who had been flirting with *her*. I'd been watching them all night, and I could tell that when Patricia told him that Rose had said they were just friends, he hadn't liked it. Figured he couldn't wait to discuss it with her until after closing.

The fire in her eyes, even behind those glasses, reminded me of Addy. When pushed, Addy had that same fire. That same determination. My chest ached. It always ached when I remembered her, and Rose made me remember all the damn time. The memories were only getting worse. There was no gun in my hand and no revenge in my plans now. I'd left that life behind.

And my mind was once again open to the good parts of my life. The best part. Even though we'd been living through hell in that house with my parents, Addy had made it perfect. She had made everything worth it. I had thought I was saving her, but she'd saved me. She'd given me a purpose. She'd shown me what real love felt like.

Then, after all she'd given me, I'd failed her in the end. I hadn't saved her after all. Loving me was what had killed her. Finding Addy and me in bed together had sent my insane mother over the edge. It hadn't been our first time—Addy had given me her innocence months before, and it had been the most beautiful moment of my life. Our time together had brought us closer and forged a bond that I thought could never be broken. In a way, I'd been right; Addy's hold on me was still there. Still strong.

"Shit, looks ace out there. No need for you to be in here scowling." Major's voice brought me out of my thoughts.

I focused on the man in front of me and shoved my memories and my issues with Rose aside. "I'm ready to move on. This ain't my thing," I said simply. Because it wasn't. I needed more solitude.

Major cocked his head and studied me. "You saying you want to come back? DeCarlo would shit a brick, he'd be so happy."

"No. Said I was finished, and I am."

Major shrugged. "Got it. But it's exciting. That thrill you get. The hunt. You don't miss that?"

He might have looked like a pretty-boy player who was always ready for a good laugh, but Major Colt was a fucked-up dude. Maybe not as fucked-up as Cope, who I wasn't sure even had a soul, but at least you knew what you were getting with Cope. Major could fool anyone. Even his own family. Which he did, brilliantly.

I glanced around, making sure we were still alone, before replying. "I did it to survive, not because I enjoyed it. I was seeking something I never truly found."

Major smirked. "So you're saying I'm a sick fuck."

"Yeah," I said.

Major chuckled. "Naw, just like the game."

Life wasn't a game. It was a gift. And choosing to take that gift from another person wasn't easy. What we did—what he did—would never be right. Didn't mean I'd change it. Every time I pulled a trigger, I knew the costs. I knew what it meant. And although I wasn't God, and choosing who got to live or die wasn't my job, I chose anyway. I corrected the wrong shit in the world, hoping each time that I was saving someone's Addy.

"Why are you still here? Job should be done," I said, moving past Major and toward the door.

"It's complicated. This one ain't cut and dry. DeCarlo wants some answers first. Lucky me, I get to fuck around with a smoking-hot babe to get those answers. God, I love this job."

I stopped at the door. "I'm leaving here soon. But I want you out and DeCarlo's job done before I go. Don't want this shit near my sister and her family. Forget about the pussy, and focus on the task."

I didn't wait for his response before I opened the door to go back out into the dining room.

"You think Mase told Reese about what DeCarlo did?" Major asked in a low voice.

I paused. I'd wondered that myself. She was one of the reasons I had been in Texas before I came to Rosemary Beach. I didn't talk to Reese now that my job for her was done, but Mase and I touched base every once in a while. Killing the man who had molested and raped Reese when she was a child had been one of my greatest moments of success. He'd ruined a young woman's life with his sickness. I would have done anything to make sure he never touched another girl. DeCarlo was her real father, and he had wanted that man's death more than anyone. His daughter had been a fighter. She had made it through hell, then walked right into the arms of Mase Colt Manning. A guy who would cherish and love her for the rest of her life. She'd been one of the lucky ones.

"No. I think if he'd told her, DeCarlo would know."

Major nodded. "Yeah."

I didn't wait for more. I went to check on the dining room. I needed tonight to be a success so I could leave and figure out the rest of my life.

Arthur was happy. Customers were happy. And I was fucking glad it was over. Soon this place would be handed over to Arthur's friend's son, Jamieson Tynes. All I had to do was train him over the next few weeks and then let him have it.

It was well after midnight before I locked up my office and headed toward the back exit. The thought of my bed had never seemed so damn good. Today had started before dawn and hadn't slowed down once.

"Captain," Elle called out, and I jerked my gaze over to see her standing just outside the dining room. I'd been doing my best to stay the hell away from her.

"Yeah," I replied in a no-nonsense tone. I didn't want any drama with her. Especially not tonight.

"Can we talk?"

"No."

"Seriously, this is how you're going to be? We slept together for weeks. We were in a relationship. You can't just turn off those emotions like that."

I stopped and made myself acknowledge her with an irritated glance. "I have no emotions, Elle. I told you that in the beginning, just like I told you I was just in it for the fucking. Nothing more."

"Who are you in love with, then? Huh? Where is she?" Elle raised her voice and took a step toward me. "If she's so damn wonderful, why isn't she here fighting for you? Because I'm here. I *do* love you. She doesn't, or she would be here."

The emotion I didn't feel for Elle was surpassed by the emotion that always came with any mention of the girl I loved. The one who owned my heart in a way no one else ever would. "She was nothing like you. She was pure and kind. She was selfless, and when she smiled, the world lit up. She was my best friend. My reason for getting up in the morning. That is who the fuck she was. No one will compete with that. Ever."

Elle threw up her hands like I was a madman. "Do you hear yourself? You're talking about her in the past tense. She's gone. You even know it. Move on! She obviously has."

I hated her in that moment. I hated her voice. I hated the way she looked. I hated the air she breathed. I wanted her to shut the fuck up. My body tensed with fury, and I had to fight the urge to bury my fist in the wall. And I couldn't roar in rage at her to get out of my sight. I couldn't lose my cool here. Not now.

All of the disgust and hate I felt toward her was contained in the glare I leveled on her. She would see it, and if she was as smart as I thought she was, she'd never come near me again.

"She's dead."

Saying those words was never easy. I wanted to throw shit. Anything but admit it out loud.

I didn't wait for her response, but the pale color of her face told me she got it. I left her behind and went to my only safe haven: my boat.

Eleven years ago

My mother was singing in the kitchen. That was never a good sign. I stopped at the door and put my hand protectively in front of Addy. It was a reflex. As if my mother would hear us and come running like a crazy person and attack her. I knew that wouldn't happen, but I was also bracing both of us for what this could mean. My mother singing meant she was happy, and that usually meant she thought my dad would be home early for dinner.

My dad never came home for dinner. He hadn't in more than four years, ever since he started sleeping with his secretary. Even now that he had a child with this other woman and spent most of his nights with his other family, my mother still pretended that wasn't the case.

I spotted the empty bottle of tequila on the coffee table and looked at Addy, who was staring at it, too. This was definitely another bad sign. My mother acting crazy was one thing. My mother crazy drunk was another.

"Go to your room, and lock the door," I whispered to her.

She looked up at me with those big eyes of hers. There was fear there, but there was also determination. She shook her head. "I won't leave you alone with her. If I lock myself in, you know she'll come after me, and you'll fight her, and she'll hit you."

I was taller than my mother now and stronger. Her hitting me didn't hurt. But her hitting Addy could break her. I wasn't letting that happen ever again. When I had made the mistake of staying after school to try out for the basketball team, Addy had come home to my drunk mother and ended up with a broken wrist. I still hadn't forgiven myself.

"It doesn't hurt me when she hits me. But I won't let her hurt you," I said quietly. I didn't want her to hear us. I wanted Addy safely locked in first.

She finally sighed in defeat and nodded. "OK. But if she starts to attack you, I'm coming out."

"No, Addy. Please. For me, stay in there. I'll hurt her if I have to." I didn't want to hurt my mother. I hated her for how she treated Addy. I hated her because she couldn't be normal and be a mother. But I didn't want to physically hurt her. I just wanted to get us the hell away from her. I also knew that if I hurt her, she'd make me pay by sending Addy away. Without me, Addy had no one to protect her the next time. I had to keep her safe.

"I love you," she whispered to me, her eyes full of unshed tears.

We had been saying that for a while now, although I thought it meant something different to her. I was in love with Addy, but she didn't look at me the same way. She never flirted or tried to get my attention the way other girls did. I couldn't help it, though. Somewhere along the way, she went from my best friend to the person I wanted to be with forever. We were young, but the shit I'd dealt with had made me grow up fast. It had done that for both of us. I knew what I felt. Addy owned me. She just didn't realize it.

"Love you, too," I replied, then nodded my head toward the steps leading up to our rooms. "Now, go. I'll handle her. You stay locked in there."

Addy gave me one last pleading look, but I pointed to the stairs, firm in my decision. Finally, she turned and quietly made her way to the bedroom that had once been a small office for my father. We had another guest bedroom that Addy could have been given, but my mother had moved her into the smallest room in the house. I often wondered if it was because it was the farthest room from mine.

With her door closed and locked behind her, I made my way to the kitchen to face my drunk and insane mother.

My mother's hair was washed and freshly rolled. She was wearing a sundress and a pair of heels while she stirred something on the stove. There was another bottle of tequila sitting on the bar to her left, and a wineglass beside it full of the liquor. She was singing some old song she called her and Dad's song. I knew tonight was going to be a bad one.

"What are you cooking?" I asked, hoping that distracting her from Addy's absence would work. Announcing that I was home would only remind her of Addy, and lately, she hated Addy more and more.

She spun around. The black mascara running down her very made-up face wasn't surprising. When she drank tequila, she usually cried. A lot. "Chicken and dumplings. The baby loves chicken and dumplings," she said, smiling.

Shit. She was back on the baby thing again. Ever since Dad had a baby with the secretary, Mom would sometimes pretend that she and Dad had a baby, too. It was so fucking wacked. I'd told Dad and asked him to get Addy and me out of the house and get Mom some help, but he always blew me off. He didn't believe it was this bad. Yet he never came home to see just how crazy his wife had become. All Dad did was pay the bills and keep money in Mom's account.

"I've got homework. I'll leave you to it. You and the baby enjoy the chicken and dumplings," I said. If I played along, she usually stayed calm. It was when I tried to snap her out of it that she lost her shit.

"We will. You'll come have some with us when Dad gets home," she called out behind me.

"Yeah, sure will."

Then the sobbing began, and I froze. Shit. This never ended well.

Rose

I wasn't a quitter, but I'd thrown down the gauntlet last night in my moment of anger, and now I had to stick with it. Then I had to find another job. Pulling up to the restaurant, I turned and looked at Franny. I had to take her to her dentist appointment today. "You stay here. Lock the doors. I'll be right back," I told her, before getting out.

"I wish I could come inside and see it," she said, studying the outside of the place. It really was a nice building. Arthur Stout hadn't cut any corners, that was for sure.

"I know, and I'm sorry. But it's not a good time," I explained. I didn't want to tell her I was quitting. Not yet. I needed to find another job first. My little girl could be a worrier.

I closed the door and waited until she locked it, then headed for the entrance. I needed to drop off my letter of resignation. I figured I wouldn't get a good reference from him anyway, but I still wanted to do this properly.

"Thought you were quitting," Captain's voice called out, and I spun around to see him getting out of his truck. I hadn't seen him parked there, but I'd been focused on my task at hand.

I held up my resignation letter. "I am. Just came to give you this." I kept my spine stiff. He had no idea of the hopes and dreams he had shattered. Not just mine but Franny's. She'd never know her dad now, because I didn't trust him to be the man she needed.

I couldn't see his expression behind his sunglasses, but at this point, I didn't care. I knew how detached and cold he was. He'd probably throw the paper into the trash as soon as he got inside and never think of me again.

"You sure you want to do this?" he asked, surprising me.

I paused. Why was he asking that? He'd been mad at me last night for something I hadn't done. "You aren't a fair boss. You don't like me, and I'm not sure why. I work hard, and I try my best to be as professional as I can. But last night you were—"

"Wrong," he finished for me. "I was wrong."

I closed my mouth, then opened it again, before closing it one more time. I didn't know what to say to that. I'd seen this side of Captain before, when he'd apologized about being hard on me when Franny was sick. But I hadn't seen it since then.

"Listen, Rose, I'm not going to be here much longer. The place is open now, and I'll be training the new manager over the next few weeks. We have a rub between us, but you're a good worker. The place needs you. Just because we don't . . . work well together, that doesn't mean you won't work great with the new guy. Stay. Give it a chance."

He was leaving soon? What? "Where are you going?" I asked, completely ignoring the fact that he'd just asked me to stay.

He shrugged. "Don't know yet. Just not here."

It shouldn't matter. But somehow it did. Quitting was one

thing, but knowing where he was helped. I couldn't change the fact that I wanted to know that River was safe and OK. I had made it through ten years of not knowing where he was, and every day I worried and hoped that he was happy.

Knowing he had become this man who was so different from the boy I had loved was hard, but at least I knew where he was. That he had family here. I wanted to have that peace. If he left, I'd lose that again. And just because my River had become Captain, that didn't change the fact that I cared. I would always care, because I would always love River. He was a part of me.

"You look really upset about that, Rose. Any particular reason?" Captain drawled, as if he were amused.

I forced myself to snap out of it and shake my head no. There was no way I could explain it to him. Even if I tried, there was a good chance he'd hate me for having left him without an explanation all those years ago. If he rejected Franny, well, I couldn't deal with that. So I said nothing.

"Mommy, I need to use the restroom," Franny's voice called out, and I turned away from Captain to look back at my daughter. She had stepped out of the car and was looking at me with an apologetic frown.

"OK, yeah." I turned back to Captain but he wasn't looking at me. His focus was on Franny. "I need to take her inside to use the restroom. Is that OK?" I asked.

He didn't reply. Instead, he stood there frozen. I wasn't even sure he was breathing. Not one muscle of his body moved. His focus was locked on Franny.

She shuffled her feet and watched us. The small smile on her lips as she met my gaze hit me hard. Oh, God. I hadn't thought about that.

"Please," she added, waiting for me to answer.

My heart was slamming against my chest, as I felt a mixture of anxiety and fear prickle my skin. This wasn't how it was supposed to happen. Not in front of Franny. Not now.

"I promise I'm not making this up just to see the inside," Franny added, as she started walking toward me. "I mean, I want to see it, but I really need to go."

Her blond curls, so like my own natural hair, bounced as she walked, and her smile looked almost identical to my own. Her blue eyes danced with mischief, and all I could do was hope he didn't see it, too.

Turning back to him, I could see even through the sunglasses he was wearing that he was following her every move. This wasn't the way a man reacted to seeing a nine-year-old girl he didn't know. He saw me—his Addy—in her.

Franny's hand wrapped around mine and squeezed. She smiled up at the silent man watching her. "Hi. I'm Franny. Do you work with Mom like Brad does?" she asked innocently.

There was a flinch at the mention of Brad, and his gaze finally moved from Franny to me. I felt exposed. I needed to cover up or hide. He was seeing too much, and I wasn't sure if he'd even put it together. Did I want him to?

"Who are you?" He finally spoke, his voice gravelly.

"I'm Ann Frances, but everyone calls me Franny. Who are you?"

The innocence in her answer made my eyes sting and my stomach tighten. This was not how it was supposed to come out. Not like this.

I squeezed Franny's hand. "Go through those doors right there, and turn right. You'll see the restroom sign on your left."

She nodded, before hurrying inside to see exactly what she wanted to see.

Once she was gone, I turned back to look at Captain.

"Who are *you*, Rose?" he asked.

Who did he think I was? If he saw the similarities between Franny and the girl I once was, then couldn't he see beyond my hair color, glasses, and mature body to see me, too? "Not sure what you mean," I replied carefully.

Captain took a deep breath and looked past me toward the building. "Is that your daughter?"

"Yes."

He moved his gaze back to mine. "Then who are you?"

I wasn't giving him that. "You have all my info on file," I reminded him.

He pulled off his sunglasses, and his eyes narrowed slightly as he studied me. I tried not to hold my breath, but I couldn't help it. There was a part of me that wanted him to see me. But the part of me that knew he wasn't my River anymore wanted to remain hidden. Not just for Franny's sake but also for my own.

River had wanted to protect me, but this man . . . I wasn't sure how I'd survive him. He could break me in a way I wouldn't recover from.

"Take off the glasses." Captain's words sounded like an order, although his voice was just above a whisper.

I stared up at him. This time, I was frozen. Did he see me now? Was that it? If I took off the glasses, it was over. He'd know, and then what? Would I just gamble on him accepting Franny? Accepting that I'd been hiding my identity all these years?

"This place is so cool!" Franny's excited voice called out.

I couldn't have been more relieved to see her. Turning from his intense gaze, I headed toward my daughter, hoping the smile I'd pasted on my face was enough for her to get into the car without any questions. "We're going to be late for the dentist. We need to go," I told her, as calmly as I could manage. I could barely contain the edge of panic in my voice.

"I hate the dentist," Franny grumbled, her excitement suddenly vanishing as she remembered where we were headed.

"But you want to keep your teeth," I reminded her, like I always did. I was more than aware of the set of eyes following our every move, but although the heat from his stare could be felt against every inch of my body, I didn't look back. I kept walking to the car, praying he would just let us go.

Franny turned and waved at him, and I shut my eyes tightly, wishing my daughter wasn't so damn friendly sometimes. She climbed back into the car, and I did the same.

My prayer was answered. He let us go.

Captain

I went straight to the employee files and pulled out the folder for Rose Henderson. I read over her personal information, her past jobs, and her address. She'd received a GED. There was no mention of college in her file. She'd been working since she was eighteen and had excellent references from all of her former employers. Especially the elementary school in Oklahoma where she had recently worked as a secretary.

But this was all bullshit.

Pulling my cell phone out of my pocket, I dialed Benedetto DeCarlo's private line.

"Cap," was his only greeting.

"I need info on someone, ASAP," I told him.

"OK. Who?"

"Her name is Rose Henderson. I'm going to scan her file and send it to you now. I need everything you can find on her."

"I'll put my men on it," he replied.

"Not your men, you. I want just you checking on this. No one else."

DeCarlo was quiet a moment. "Going to tell me why?"

"I think . . . I fucking think . . ." What did I think? That little girl had looked just like Addy, but what did that even mean? Addy was gone. So who was Rose? "I think she's con-nected to *her*." I knew he'd understand. There was only one *her* in my life who had ever mattered.

"I'll have your info within the next few hours," he said be-fore we disconnected.

Once I had the file scanned and sent to DeCarlo, I sank into my chair and stared at the paperwork in my hands. So many similarities. Was I grasping at something in desperation? Yes, Rose had Addy's laugh, and when she smiled, I sometimes felt like I'd been kicked in the stomach. Those could have been coincidences, but the little girl looked like Addy. So goddamn much like Addy that I hadn't been able to speak at first. She was younger than the Addy I'd first met, but she still looked so much like her. It had been hard to breathe.

The look on Rose's face had screamed that she was hiding something. Hell, she'd practically run away from me. There was something to that. I knew there was. I wasn't making this shit up. Who the hell was Rose Henderson?

I wasn't good at waiting. I'd memorized every word on Rose's job application. I had gone over every conversation I'd ever had with her. The night my dreams about Addy had returned was after the first time I'd heard Rose laugh. Then it turned out that her daughter looked exactly like Addy. There was a con-nection. There had to be a fucking connection.

No one here knew Rose. Except, possibly, Brad. I was ir-rationally angry with him at the moment, because he was close to someone who was somehow connected to Addy. It made no sense, but I didn't like it. I wanted him away from her.

But right now, I wanted to know what he knew about Rose. Maybe she'd said something to him that could be a clue. I headed straight for the kitchen, knowing he was in there working. The moment the door swung open, Brad looked up.

"We need to talk," I said, before he could start telling me about some new entrée he wanted to try or how well another one was doing. The man always talked about food.

"OK," he said, with a slight frown, as he set down his knife and wiped his hands on the towel hanging at the waist of his jeans.

"It's about Rose. Can you meet me in my office?" I didn't want anyone else overhearing this.

Brad's eyes went wide, and he nodded. "Sure. She OK?"

"Yeah," I replied in a clipped tone.

I went back to my office, Brad following me.

Once he closed the door behind him, I didn't wait for him to ask anything else. This was my time for questions. "Where is Rose from? Did she ever mention it?"

Brad's frown grew deeper, and then he shook his head. "No," he said.

"She ever talk about any family other than her daughter?"

"She doesn't have any family. She was a foster kid." He said the words as if they were a simple fact. The impact of them, however, burst open the tight hold I had on something I didn't want to believe.

"Foster kid," I repeated, but it wasn't a question.

"Yeah, she said she left the system when she was sixteen because of a bad situation. Won't talk about anything else, though. She shuts down pretty fast."

I sat on the edge of my desk and gripped the sides of it in

both hands to keep from screaming out in relief or rage or . . . fuck if I knew what was happening to me right now. This wasn't real. I couldn't believe this.

"She do something wrong? She's a really good, genuine person, Captain. Great mom. And a single mom, at that. Never been married."

I wanted to be alone so I could call DeCarlo. But I had one more question. "How old is her daughter?"

"Nine."

Fuck me.

Addy

When we got home and I saw that Captain's truck wasn't in the drive, I knew it wouldn't be long before it would be. I took Franny over to visit with Mrs. Baylor and explained that I would be having company later, making sure that Franny could stay until I came for her.

Mrs. Baylor had looked concerned, but then I was battling anxiety, fear, and uncertainty so fiercely that hiding it was impossible. Getting Franny safely tucked away and dealing alone until Captain showed up was best. I had to come to a decision.

Captain knew something. He was connecting the dots. It was very likely he did recognize me but hated me so badly that he had let me leave. But I knew enough about the man he'd become to know he was going to want more answers. I expected his questions sooner rather than later.

I hadn't been back at the house for an hour before his truck pulled into the driveway. When I heard the crunch of seashells under the tires, I knew without looking that it was him. I waited at my kitchen table while he made his way to the door.

His footsteps stopped, and he waited a moment before he knocked. This was it. Time for the truth. I'd deal with the consequences and keep Franny as protected as possible.

Standing up, I took a deep breath and tried to calm my beating heart, then took off my glasses and laid them on the table. There was no point in wearing them now. When I came here, I knew this day would come. I'd prepared for it several times over the past year. But I realized now that you could never truly prepare for something like this.

Our past wasn't normal, yet neither was the way I loved River Kipling. He'd been my anchor in the storm until I had needed to break free to save him. And I had. Because I'd loved him that much.

As I opened the door, every memory I had of River flooded through me. Every good moment, every life-changing moment, every time he had made me feel safe. I owed it to that boy to answer to this man. To give him the truth. All of it.

Eleven years ago

I sat curled up on my bed while tears silently slid down my cheeks. My stupid, freckled cheeks. I hated having freckles. I hated being short. I wanted to be tall and tan, like Delany O'Neil. Then maybe River would look at me the way he looked at her.

I squeezed my eyes shut tightly, trying to fight back the image in my head from today. River was supposed to be waiting for me to walk me home, but he wasn't there yet. I figured since I'd gotten out of class early, I could go find him and meet him on his way out. I wanted to tell him I passed the history test he helped me study for.

It hadn't been hard to find him. He had Delany O'Neil pressed up against his locker, his hands on her breasts and his mouth glued to hers. I even saw a glimpse of her tongue—or his, I wasn't sure.

It was hard to take it all in when my heart exploded into a million pieces in my chest.

Delany had her hands tangled in River's sun-kissed locks that I always wanted to touch but never did. Her leg was sliding up to his hip, and when he moved a hand to grab her thigh, I couldn't take the pain anymore. I covered my mouth to silence my cry and turned and ran home.

The house was empty. I was thankful I didn't have to worry about a beating or punishment just for being alive. My room was the only comfort I wanted. Locked inside, alone. Me and my heartbreak.

I knew River liked Delany. I'd seen him watch her when she walked by. He was beautiful, and it was only a matter of time before she turned his way. He'd be in love with her soon. He'd want to be with her, and I'd be left here alone.

At least I wouldn't have to worry about him getting hurt or having to see his mother act crazy. He would get a break from that when he was with Delany. I'd just need to learn to live with it and survive it while he was gone. It wasn't like I'd have him around to protect me forever.

The doorknob turned, and I jumped before the banging began. "Addy, are you in there?" River's voice was panicked. I hadn't told him I was leaving, but I figured he'd forget about me with Delany latched onto him.

"Yeah," I croaked out, wincing at the sound of my own voice.

"Shit, are you OK? Why did you come back without me? Did she hurt you? Fuck, Addy, open the door."

He was worried about me. He was always worried about me. I was his burden, and I hated that even more than I hated my freckles. I sniffled and wiped at my face, knowing it was going to be red and splotchy.

"Please, Addy. Open up," he begged.

I stood and went to the door, wishing I didn't have to face him. I could still see his hand on Delany and his tongue in her mouth. Cringing with jealousy and disgust, I opened the door.

River shoved inside before I could get it all the way open. "What happened?" he asked, cupping my face and studying it closely for any signs of abuse.

"Nothing," I mumbled, and stepped away from him, knowing where those hands had been so recently. "You see, I'm good. You can go." I pointed to the door without making eye contact with him.

"Like hell you're good. You won't even look at me, and since when do you kick me out of your room? Addy, something happened, and I want to know who the fuck I need to beat up." He was always ready to save me. The short, freckled best friend who was in love with him.

"No one. It's not what you think. I'm just emotional," I admitted. I walked back to my bed to sit down.

"You're never emotional. Something's wrong. Tell me."

He didn't realize that he didn't really want to know what was wrong. He thought he did, but he really didn't. How would he handle it? I wasn't a girl he could avoid. I was in his house. Living the same daily hell he was. "Would you trust me if I told you that you don't want to know this, and you can't fix it?" I asked him.

He shook his head no. "I want to know what makes you cry, because I know I can fucking fix it."

Sighing, I pulled my knees up under my chin and turned my head away from him to stare at the wall. We would do this all night. He wouldn't leave until I told him. He'd know if I lied to him, because he could read me too well. In so many ways, we were similar. Telling him was going to hurt us both. But he was my best friend, and if I was going to have a hard time adjusting to this, then he should be prepared. I doubted this was the last time I would curl up and cry over him and Delany. Or some other girl.

"I saw you with Delany," I whispered. As soon as I said it, I wished I hadn't. I hoped he hadn't heard me. When he didn't respond, I thought maybe I had a reprieve and he had missed the admission. Closing my eyes tightly, I held my breath.

"That's why you're crying?" he asked, too gently, in a tone that told me he cared. It only made me feel worse. He would hate to think he had made me cry. I'd been selfish to tell him. "Addy, talk to me. Is that why you left school without me and why you're crying right now?"

River was fifteen. He was popular at school, and although he didn't play sports (once again, because of me), people still loved him. Was it so wrong that I'd fallen in love with him, too?

His hand touched my arm, and I jumped, but I wouldn't look at him. I felt so guilty. It was my fault he didn't play sports, and now I was making him think he couldn't date or I'd cry like a baby.

"I'm sorry. Just ignore this. I swear I'll never react this way again," I said, with as much conviction as I could. I wanted him to believe me.

"Answer me, Addy. Are you crying over what you saw? Me and Delany?"

I shuddered, hating to hear her name with his. But she was tall and beautiful and popular. They made sense. They fit.

River sat down beside me, keeping his hand on my arm. "That's it. That's why you're crying. Because you saw me with Delany, and it upset you."

He wasn't asking questions now. He was stating what he'd figured out from my silence.

"Why does that upset you?" he asked. His voice was a low rumble as he moved closer to me and his thumb caressed my arm. "You've always talked to me before. Don't stop now. I need you to tell me, Addy. Please. Talk to me." The desperate plea in his voice was my undoing. I was hurting him, and he didn't deserve it.

I turned my gaze to his, and my eyes held more unshed tears. "I'm sorry. I . . . I know we're friends, and I know you would do anything for me. So this is unfair, and I don't want to tell you, because I don't want you to feel bad for me."

River didn't move. His eyes pleaded with me to continue, so I did.

"I was jealous. It was hard to see . . ." I swallowed against the lump in my throat. "I didn't want . . . I don't want . . ." I closed my eyes. I couldn't say it and look at him. "I don't want to hurt our friendship, but I'm in love with you." There. I had said it.

Before I could think of anything else, River's hands were once again cupping my face, but this time, it was different. There was an intimacy to it that didn't come when he was checking me for bruises. "Look at me, Addy."

Slowly, I opened my eyes and stared into his. There was so much emotion there. I wasn't able to read him and know what he was feeling.

"I've been in love with you for a while now. I just didn't think you felt that way about me."

"What?" I said, confused.

He gave me a grin, then moved in closer. "I'm in love with you. You're all I care about."

Frowning, I looked down and tried to move my face away, but he held on to me with a firm yet gentle touch. "I saw you caring a lot about Delany."

"No, what you saw was me being a guy. I didn't think you felt more than friendship for me, so when Delany came on to me, I took the chance. I don't love her. She loves herself enough. She was just a distraction."

"What?" I repeated. "You . . . you touched her breasts and her thigh. I saw your tongue in her mouth."

River winced as if that pained him. "I hate that you saw that. But I'll never do it again. I swear to God. If you love me, Addy, then I'm yours. I've been yours for years."

Captain

She wasn't wearing her glasses, and without those large frames covering her face, I could see her eyes clearly. Eyes that had haunted me for years. She had changed her hair color, but that was Addy's face. Just the grown-up version. How had I missed it?

Because I hadn't believed she was alive. I'd never looked at her hoping to see Addy.

"Addy," I said, simply needing her to assure me that I wasn't hallucinating and this was real. She was real.

She stepped back from the door so I could come inside. "River," she replied simply, and that was the only answer I needed.

All the questions I'd had on my way over here, when I was still afraid to believe that Rose was Addy, vanished. I couldn't form words. The best thing I could manage was "How?"

Addy closed the door once I was inside and turned to look at me. "How what? How did I find you?"

Find me? She'd been looking for me? It had been ten years. I shook my head. Yes, I wanted that answer, too, but first . . . "How are you alive?"

She frowned and studied me a moment, as if my question made no sense.

Did she not think that would be the first thing I'd want to know? Fuck, I'd thought she was dead for ten years of hell. If I'd had any idea she was alive, I'd have come after her. Found her. I had that kind of power with DeCarlo. Finding her would have been easy, but I'd seen what my mother had done to her.

"I don't understand the question. I left without a word because I was protecting you from your mother. From me and the fate you'd be handed if I stayed. I saved us both, really. Why would you think I was dead?"

"Why would you leave? You knew you didn't have to save me. I kept you safe, Addy, not the other way around. And I thought you were dead because my mother came home with a gun in her hands and blood on her clothes. She admitted to killing you and throwing your body into a lake, but she wouldn't disclose the exact location. You never came home. I hoped she was lying, but you never came back. You never contacted me. I went to the police, and Mom was arrested and sent to a mental hospital, where she eventually took her own life. Fuck, Addy, I had every damn body of water in a hundred-mile radius dragged as soon as I had the money and power to do it. I wanted you properly buried." My heart was pounding in my chest as I let the memories and the pain wash over me. But seeing her standing here was almost too much.

"The blood was mine," she said quietly. But I knew that already. The cops had confirmed it. "She checked me out of school that day. I had asked the office to please call you to the office, but she'd been on her best behavior and explained that she didn't want you disturbed because of my doctor's appointment. So I went, although I knew there was no doctor's appointment.

"She took me out of town and parked at the back of a parking lot at a bus station. Then she asked me how many times we'd had sex. I didn't want to tell her. That crazy look was in her eyes, and I knew if I told her, she'd lose it. So I said once. She hit me across the face and busted my lip. Then she asked me again, and I told her three times. She hit me again. Then she asked me again. This went on five times, even though my answer stayed the same. I was bleeding badly by this time, and she shoved money at me and told me to get on a bus and leave and never come back. That I could be pregnant with your brat, and I wasn't going to taint her name and yours.

"She said what we had done was dirty, and she wouldn't have it. If I didn't leave, she'd send me back into the system, and if I was pregnant, they'd take my baby away from me. My period was late. I hadn't told you because I wasn't sure if it was a concern yet, but hearing her tell me I'd end up losing not only you but our baby was enough to terrify me.

"I took the money and had started to get out of the car when she grabbed my arm and twisted it until I cried out. Then she said if I ever tried to contact you, she'd kill us both. I believed her. But when I could afford to check into things a couple of years later, I found out she was in a mental hospital. I just couldn't find River Kipling anywhere. I never stopped looking, though."

Fuck. I sat there listening to Addy's words and not once questioning them. My mother had been insane, but I never once thought she had let Addy go. That she'd scared her and sent her running. I always thought her insanity had taken Addy's life.

"You were just sixteen," I whispered, afraid to hear how she'd survived and if Franny . . . if Franny was mine.

Addy nodded, but her face stayed tense. "It wasn't easy. I was in a homeless shelter, getting a free meal, when the smell of turnip greens made me sick. The minister's wife who had been helping to serve food immediately came to my side and helped me get cleaned up. Deborah Posey was my savior. She found out I was sixteen and alone and took me into her home. She bought me the pregnancy test that confirmed I was pregnant. I wanted to call you then, but the fear of losing you and the baby . . . I couldn't do that to either of you.

"Deborah let me stay with her family until I started showing and we couldn't hide it. They were Southern Baptist, and the congregation wouldn't accept a pregnant teenage girl living in the minister's home. So she helped get me a job in Oklahoma, where her sister lived, and it was there that I made a life for Franny and me."

Hating my mother had been something I'd accepted a long time ago. I'd hated my father just as fiercely, though, because he had left us with her. He hadn't helped her. But now, knowing Addy had lived through this hell made me hate the woman who gave me life even more. So many things could have happened to Addy. So many bad things, and I hadn't been there.

"She's mine." I needed to say it aloud. I had known Franny was mine, but hearing Addy say it made it real.

She just nodded.

I had a daughter.

But the woman in front of me was a stranger now. The girl I'd loved once and known better than anyone was now distant and reserved. She was strong and independent. She didn't need me anymore. She also didn't seem to like me very much. We were strangers, and the pang that came with that realization sliced through me.

When I didn't say anything, Addy moved toward the small living room. "Why don't we sit down? I can get you a drink."

I hadn't moved from the spot where I was standing. Addy was so much calmer about everything. But then, she'd been here watching me, knowing who I was, for more than a month. She'd had time to adjust. I followed her and sat on the first chair I came to, but I couldn't stop looking at her. I should have seen it. The first fucking day she walked into the restaurant.

"Your hair," I said, with more accusation in my voice than necessary, but dammit, she had hidden herself from me. She had been hiding right fucking in front of me.

She touched the darker locks and gave me a small smile. "I didn't want to walk into your world as Addy. I needed to be sure that the man you had become was someone I wanted Franny to know. She's been asking about her father for years, and I've been looking. When I found you, I didn't want to bring her into your life until I knew you'd accept her and she wouldn't be hurt."

As pissed as I was, I got it. She was a loving, protective mother. Something she'd never had in her own life. Something neither of us had had.

The fact that she hadn't intentionally kept my kid from me eased the anger some, but I still felt robbed. Losing Addy had sent me on a course that had molded me into a man who was nothing like the boy who had loved her. I wasn't the guy she had left behind.

"I'm different. I've done things that have changed me," I said, looking at her as she sat down across from me.

She gave me a tight smile and looked away. "I know you're different. I've seen it."

Those words made me feel like I'd failed. I had fought to survive. She knew nothing of what I'd endured. I knew her life had been hard, but mine hadn't been easy, either. There was no minister's wife to help me. I had killed men. I had lost my fucking soul because her death had ruined me.

"I want to know my daughter." I wasn't going to let her keep Franny from me. If she wasn't happy with the man she saw, that wasn't OK with me. I had a right to know my child. To be involved in her life.

Addy swung her gaze back to me. "Good. She wants to know her father."

Eleven years ago

I knocked once on Addy's door. Mom was passed out drunk, but I was still careful not to make enough noise to disturb her. I wanted her to remain passed out. Addy had stayed hidden in her room, like I told her to, all evening. We hadn't even gotten to talk about the day. Plus, I just wanted to be near her. She was letting me hold her hand at school now, and last night, she'd let me hold her until she fell asleep. I wanted more of that.

The door opened slowly, and Addy gave me a shy smile before stepping back and letting me in. Being near her, knowing I could touch her, made me feel a little off balance. I wanted so much, but I didn't want to scare her. I didn't want to lose what I had been given. My heart always beat faster when she was near.

"I just finished my homework," she said, walking over to the bed to put away her books.

Her blond hair fell over her shoulder. I wanted to play with her hair. Run my fingers through it and watch the way it looked sliding over my hand. "You don't need help with anything?" I asked.

She set the books on the small table beside the bed and shook her head no. "Not tonight." Then she sat down and patted the spot beside her. "You look ready to bolt. What's wrong?"

Shit. I was messing it up because I couldn't stay calm around her. My imagination was running wild. I had to control this. "I'm good. Just wasn't sure if you wanted me to stay tonight or not." God, let her say yes.

She grinned and ducked her head. "I always want you to stay," she said softly.

My heart slammed against my ribs, and I took a deep breath. Calm. I had to stay fucking calm. I moved over to sit beside her. "So how was school today?" I asked, hoping I didn't sound as wound-up as I was.

She scooted closer to me, and her hand slipped over mine. "It was good. Same as every other day."

I turned my hand over so that our palms were touching and threaded my fingers through her small ones. Even her pale skin against my tanned skin turned me on. This was going to kill me. I wanted so much of her, and I had to stop thinking about how soft and sweet the skin under her clothes would be.

"River," she said, leaning closer toward me.

Breathe. I had to remember to breathe. "Yeah?"

"Why won't you kiss me?"

I jerked my gaze to lock with hers. "What?"

Her cheeks turned a pretty pink. "Why won't you kiss me?" she repeated. "I know you like kissing girls, but you haven't kissed me."

The crotch of my jeans got extremely tight as I looked down at her innocent, beautiful face asking me to kiss her. Like I was going to turn that down. I wasn't sure I would be able to stop when it was time and not let my hands go places she wasn't ready for.

"I was waiting until you were ready," I told her honestly.

She licked her lips, and the tip of her tongue peeked out, taunting me. "I'm ready."

This would be her first kiss and my last first kiss. Because once I did this, I'd never touch anyone else again. Just Addy.

Addy

So many times over the past ten years, I had imagined this day. When I would see River again and tell him why I ran away and tell him about Franny. Not once did it play out like this in my imagination. But then, all I'd had was the memory of River. I didn't know Captain. The man he had become was someone I didn't much care for.

But he wanted to be part of Franny's life, and she deserved that. He wasn't a bad man. He just wasn't the guy I had known. Then again, I was no longer the girl he had loved. It was hard to face, but now that I had him here as River, not my boss Captain, I had to deal with it.

"Does she know that I'm her father? Or that her father is in this town?" he asked, watching me closely, as if he was trying to determine if I was lying.

I shook my head. "She has no idea. Like I said, I needed to see who you were now before I told her." He didn't like it when I said that. I could tell by the way his eyes tightened, but I wasn't here to make friends with him. Franny came first. He needed to get that.

"When can we tell her?"

I liked that he said "we," as if he was ready to take a real role in her life. However, I was used to being the only decision maker in her life, and a part of me wasn't ready to share. "I can sit her down tonight, but I need to do that alone. Once she understands why I brought her here and wanted to wait to introduce her to you, then we can meet together. The three of us."

He nodded. I was glad he didn't argue.

We sat there in silence, not looking at each other. There was a gulf between us that I had never imagined would ever exist. He'd been my soul mate, my best friend, and I'd carried that memory of him with me all these years. It hurt simply because I knew I needed to let go of that.

Looking up from my hands, I asked him, "Why couldn't I find you, and why did you change your name?" I'd told him everything, yet he had given me nothing.

"Dad divorced Mom when she was committed, and then he married Carlotta, the secretary. I ran. Left town and didn't look back. Met a man who gave me a job and an escape. A way to deal with my demons."

That was it? He wasn't telling me anything more than that? "What did you do? Did you change your name because you ran?"

He shook his head and stood up. "I changed it because I wanted to forget what River Kipling had suffered. I wanted to start a life where that past could be forgotten." That was it. All he was going to say. Reaching out his hand, he said, "Give me your phone. I'll put my number in it."

I didn't question him. I did as he asked. He quickly added his number to my contacts and handed the phone back to me.

Standing, I waited for more, but he turned and headed for the door. I watched him until he stopped and turned to look back at me. "I'm not accepting your resignation letter. I was an ass the other night. I won't be again. It was a stressful night, and Brad deserved that correction, not you. I'll see you tomorrow evening for work. And talk to Franny. I've already lost enough time with her. Call me as soon as she's ready."

Then he opened the door and walked out without waiting for me to respond.

I had never imagined this was how tonight would end.

I walked over to the window to watch Captain get into his truck and drive away. Once he was gone, I made my way outside to get Franny from Mrs. Baylor's.

I planned to keep Franny home from school the next day. We were going to have all the time she needed to talk about Captain. I knew she'd have questions. I also knew she'd want to meet Captain officially as soon as possible. She'd been waiting a long time to meet her father.

I started making chocolate-chip pancakes, which were Franny's favorite, and texted Captain.

I'm talking to Franny today. She'll want to see you soon. Let me know when you're available.

It took him only seconds to respond.

I'll be ready when she is.

This was River. I didn't have access to him anymore, but maybe, for Franny, he would be the guy I'd once known. The protector who would do or be whatever she needed.

I trusted him. I just hoped I wasn't wrong.

"Are those chocolate chip?" Franny's sleepy voice asked. I could sense the excitement in her tone.

"Yes, they are," I replied, holding up the bag of chips.

"Yay! I'll pour the milk," she said, running over to the fridge.

"Good idea. These are almost done."

Franny concentrated on not spilling the milk, and I finished the pancakes. Once we had the table set, I glanced over at the clock, while Franny covered up a yawn and sank into a chair.

"Today we're going to hang out, just you and me. No school. How's that sound?" I said a little too brightly.

Franny studied me a moment. "Are we moving again?" she asked, with dread in her voice.

I shook my head no and smiled. "No, but I have something I want to talk to you about. A good thing. So let's eat, and then we can talk all you want."

She didn't pick up her fork. "What good thing?"

I shouldn't have mentioned it yet. She was an impatient kid. She liked knowing the ending before she read a book or watched a movie. It figured she'd want to know what the talk was about before we had it. "You eat first, then we'll talk," I replied, before taking a bite.

Franny looked down at her pancakes and gave in. She couldn't resist her favorite treat. I breathed a sigh of relief. I needed time to focus and prepare before I told my daughter that she had met her father for the first time yesterday.

Captain

I hadn't slept at all last night. When I'd gotten back to the boat, I'd grabbed a bottle of whiskey and taken several long swigs, before putting my fist through a wall. Then I'd thrown a chair and broken the leg. I'd leaned back and cradled my head in my hands while the emotions raging inside me destroyed me.

Addy is alive. We have a daughter. I'd lost all those years with both of them. I'd killed men and lost every piece of my fucking soul except for the one that still held on to the love I had for that girl. A girl who I wasn't even sure liked me anymore. Who the fuck could blame her?

I'd been an ass to her. I had fucking acted annoyed when her kid—no, *our* kid—was sick, and she had taken care of her alone. Holy fucking hell! My kid. She'd been taking care of my kid, and I had made her feel as if it were a problem. The sick knot in my stomach twisted as I remembered every conversation I'd had with her since she'd walked back into my life.

Looking into her eyes last night had been my undoing. I'd had to get the hell out of that house. Get some distance. I'd been so close to dropping to my knees and begging her to forgive me. Which might have been the best thing I could have done. But I'd been so emotionally raw I hadn't been sure I could say much more.

I pulled my phone out of my pocket again to look at the simple text she'd sent, just so I could see her name on my screen. *Addy.* My chest constricted, and I took a shallow breath. She was here. This was real.

I had lain awake so many nights, imagining what our life would be like now if I'd only been there to protect her. She was my ultimate reason in life for fighting. Every battle I fought, every wrong I righted, had been for her.

But for what? She had withdrawn from me. I had let her down. I'd killed the guy she once knew. This was me now. It was all I had left. And I'd never be enough for her. She deserved so much more.

I had been out seeking justice for others while the one person in the world I'd ever loved or cared about was struggling to make it.

I wasn't going into work until Addy called. I couldn't. Standing on my boat, holding my phone close to me, waiting for her next text, was all I could do.

Eleven years ago

My parents had been screaming at each other for more than an hour. I held Addy in my arms as we lay on her bed, quietly listening. We both wanted my dad to do something, but he never did. It didn't stop us from hoping, though.

When the door slammed, my mother's sobs grew louder, and I thought we would be in for a fight, but then she screamed, and the door slammed again as she went after him. We were alone now. The silence in the house was as peaceful as it got around here.

"Do you think she should be driving?" Addy whispered, even though no one was in the house to hear us.

"No, but I can't stop her," I replied. I probably could, but that meant bringing her back into the house and making Addy a target. I wasn't willing to do that.

"He's not coming back, is he?" she asked, and there was fear in her tone. We both knew that if this went to court, Addy would be taken out of our home and sent somewhere else. I wouldn't let them take her from me. Who knew what kind of situation she'd land in next? At least here, she had me.

"No, but I'm not letting anyone take you," I assured her.

She snuggled closer to me and tilted her head up to press a kiss to my jawline. "I love you," she said softly.

"I love you, too. Always," I replied. And I meant it. I'd love her forever.

"Promise?" she asked

"Swear to God."

That made her smile, and I loved making her smile. "Will you sleep in here with me?"

My answer was always yes. "Yeah, nowhere else I'd rather be."

She moved her hands up to squeeze my arms tightly. "Kiss me, please."

Again, another request I'd never turn down.

Her lips were so soft it made me want to be careful with them, but she always pressed harder, deepening our kisses, until I forgot to treat her like she was fragile. Her hands slid up my chest, as she grabbed fistfuls of my shirt and arched her body against me. Every curve pressed against me. The plumpness of her breasts teased me, because I hadn't touched her there yet. Not really. But God, I wanted to, and the way she was rubbing against me, I knew she wanted it, too. She was ready.

In the darkness of her room, lit only by moonlight streaming through the one small window above her dresser, we were cocooned in our safe world. The one we created to forget about the evil around us. We didn't think of our desires as being wrong. We had seen wrong, and we knew this wasn't it. The feeling was too genuine. Our hearts were leading this. I'd been with girls when it was just about lust. I knew the difference.

Slowly, I slipped a hand under her shirt, and she stilled, her breathing heavy, as I moved it up and over her bra to cup her right breast. She shuddered as I ran my thumb over the pebbled nipple pushing against the worn cotton. I needed more. Tugging down the front, I freed both breasts and moved my other hand up so I had them both full. Addy rolled onto her back and let out a small moan that made my cock jerk in reaction. Her eyes fluttered closed, and she arched her back, giving me more, and I took it. My blood was pumping so hard I could hear it as I slid her shirt off and threw it onto the floor before taking off her bra.

Her eyes opened, and she looked at me with a mix of need and uncertainty.

"You're beautiful," I told her, leaning down to press a kiss to her lips.

She opened for me so easily and wrapped her arms around me. Her hard nipples, now bare, pressed into my chest, and my cock twitched again. I began a trail of kisses down her jaw toward her neck and then spent some time on her collarbone, before moving my hands to cup each round, creamy breast. Pale pink nipples, more *perfect than anything I'd ever seen, grew even harder as my mouth moved closer, and I pulled one into my mouth.*

Addy cried out my name, and her hands went to my head and held on to my hair as she squirmed under me. Tonight I'd have to stop here, but I knew this was just the beginning. I'd been in love with Addy for a while now, but she'd just given me a taste of more. I'd never want anyone but her. This was as close to heaven as any man could get.

Addy

Franny stared at me without saying a word. I was worried that I'd rushed this or that I hadn't thought it through or that she was upset that I'd kept it from her since we'd arrived.

"So . . . he wants to meet me, too, then?" she finally asked, her eyes big with wonder. This had been her one request for so long. Having it placed in front of her had to be overwhelming. I let out the breath I was holding when I realized her silence wasn't because she was angry; she was being given something she wanted desperately.

"Yes, he does. Very much. He had no idea you existed. There was a misunderstanding that kept us apart, and it has taken me a very long time to find him. But he's glad I did. He wants to know you, too, and be a part of your life."

She scrunched her nose. "Our life, you mean?"

No . . . not ours. Just hers.

I knew that from our conversation last night and from watching him over the past few months. He wasn't interested in getting to know me. I didn't appeal to him now. The people we once were no longer existed. Not really.

"He wants to know you, sweetie. You're his child. We did love each other very much once, and you were conceived from that love. But we've grown up and changed since then. We don't have those feelings anymore."

Franny nodded as if she understood, but I could tell by the look on her face that she didn't. Not at all. When you're nine, it's hard to make sense of a lot of things. Especially things your mother has a hard time coming to terms with. "Will you be there when I see him?"

"Yes," I assured her, and she looked relieved.

"OK, when can I see him?"

I knew this would happen. Once she decided on something, she wanted it right then and there. "He said he would be ready when you are," I replied.

Franny took a deep breath and nodded her head. "I'm ready."

This was it. All those years of wondering, and this was it. River would be in his daughter's life. I had wanted this for so long. Franny deserved it. "OK." I pulled out my phone and texted Captain.

She's ready to see you.

It wasn't even thirty seconds before he replied.

Do you want me to come there, or would it be easier on her if we met for ice cream or something?

I looked up at Franny, who was watching me and chewing her bottom lip nervously.

Ice cream would be good, I think.

He replied immediately.

Meet me at the Sugar Shack when you're ready. I'll be waiting.

This was going so fast. He'd just seen Franny yesterday, and that was a total accident. Now he was meeting her and officially becoming a part of her life. I looked at my daughter.

There was a chance that this could hurt me, but I'd go through any pain for her. If I could just remember that Captain wasn't my River. Not anymore. I hoped I could trust my heart to realize what my head already did. I wasn't getting River back.

"We're going to meet him at the Sugar Shack for ice cream," I told her with a smile. She had been to the Sugar Shack once. It had been a treat when I got my first paycheck once we moved here. It was a quaint little ice cream parlor full of every candy you could imagine, right on the beach.

She clapped and jumped up. "I'll go get dressed."

I watched her run back to the bedroom and hoped I was doing the right thing. If this made her that happy, I feared I was setting her up for potential pain, too. But I had to stick with my decision. My gut said that no matter what, Captain would be there for her. He might have bad taste in women, but that was something I'd discuss with him once we were past this. Franny would have to be the most important girl in his life now.

Eleven years ago

I watched from a distance as Delany flirted with River. Because it would possibly get me kicked out of the house if a teacher noticed that River and I were a couple, we didn't act any differently at school. I wanted to hold his hand, but we both knew that if someone told his parents, they'd move me out. Then I'd be sent to a home for girls until I was eighteen. Those had terrible reputations, and I'd never see River again.

The hardest thing was watching girls flirt with River. He never flirted back, and he always kept his distance, but it was still hard to watch. I wondered if he would start to hate me because his life was so hard with me in it. I didn't want to be a burden to him, but I wasn't helpful. His mother went crazy whenever I was around, so he had to keep me away from her. I couldn't be a normal girlfriend, so he didn't get to take me to parties, which meant he didn't go to them, either.

Delany touched his chest, and I stopped breathing, watching and wishing I could walk away and trust him. But it was more than trust. I wanted to see his face. See if he wanted her, too. It was all I had to reassure me.

Those full lips of his that I loved to touch turned down in displeasure as he took her hand and removed it while backing away. I was too far from them to hear him, but he looked annoyed. The tightness in my chest that I knew was jealousy slowly faded, and I had started to turn to leave when his eyes locked with mine.

I was caught. I wished I'd left sooner. I didn't like him thinking I spied on him. That was unfair, too. He didn't need me watching his every move. The corners of his lips lifted, and he smirked at me, then started walking my way. I could run now, so I didn't have to confront him, but I'd still have to face it later.

Delany called out to him, and he didn't glance back. Her hateful gaze bored into me, before she turned on her heel and stalked off angrily. I didn't mind if she thought River was with me. She wasn't anyone who could hurt us.

"Enjoy the show?" he asked, his smirk softening with his words.

I felt my cheeks heat up and ducked my head, unable to look him in the eyes. I was guilty, and it was embarrassing. "Sorry. I was just walking by and saw you . . ." I trailed off.

His hand brushed mine, which was the only contact we dared to have at school other than talking. "You're my girl, Addy. You know that. Don't want no one else." His voice was a low, husky whisper.

My insides felt warm. Only River made me feel like that. Before him, I didn't know you could feel like a summer day was pulsing through every limb of your body, complete with sunshine and sweet lemonade.

"I know. I just . . . I was . . . I'm sorry," I said finally. There was nothing else I could say. He knew why I'd watched him. I wasn't going to lie.

River chuckled. "I figure if your girl is jealous, she wants you as much as you want her. If she stops being jealous, she wants someone else. I'll take the jealousy. It's sweet."

Smiling, I looked up into his eyes. "I was going to say I wasn't jealous, but if that's how you see it, then I was incredibly jealous." I whispered so no one else could hear me.

River winked. "Good. Because any guy who looks your way makes me see red. Let's get to class."

I walked beside him back into the hallway, with my chest so big and full of love it was a wonder it didn't explode right there.

Captain

I sat on a bench just outside the Sugar Shack, watching for Addy's car. I had gotten here ten minutes after she texted, knowing it could be an hour before they arrived, but I wasn't going to let them get here first. I wanted this. I also needed to see Addy again, because I'd been a mess last night. I'd hardly been able to speak or make sense of anything; I'd been so distracted by her sitting across from me and knowing it was her.

After breaking shit and getting out my anger and frustration at how fucking unfair our lives had turned out, I was ready to see our daughter. I was ready to see her as mine. Knowing that we'd made a child during the brightest and happiest time of our lives somehow eased the bad memories. Franny made everything that had come after worth it.

I just wished I could have been there. The life Addy and I had imagined, cuddled together in her bed, would never happen, but at least I had this. I had a part of her that was mine, too. We shared something—no, we shared *someone*. The product of the only love I'd ever experienced.

The idea that Addy might have loved again felt like a butcher knife to the gut. There had been other women for me, but I'd never given my heart to anyone else. What if she had? What if I hadn't been her only love, just her first? Could I deal with that kind of information? Fuck, no. I'd have to break more shit, because when it came to Addy, I was irrational.

I noticed her car the moment it turned onto the small street, and I stood up so she would see me. This was it. I was going to meet my daughter. It was also my chance to show Addy that I wasn't a completely cold bastard.

The car stopped in a parking spot a few feet away, and I could see all that blond hair, so much like her mother's. It stood out, just like Addy's always had. Addy turned and said something to her, and Franny nodded before they opened their doors and stepped out.

Franny's face watched me with a mixture of hope, fear, and excitement. She was as easy to read as Addy was. I was beginning to think that she'd gotten nothing from me, but to have a daughter who was the exact replica of Addy wasn't a bad thing—or at least, it wouldn't be until she was old enough to date. Then I'd have to make sure boys knew how well I handled a gun.

The thought made me scowl, and Franny halted her steps. I realized what I was doing and shook the thought away, putting a smile on my face that wouldn't scare my kid. She relaxed some and reached for her mother's hand before walking the rest of the way toward me.

I shifted my gaze to Addy, who had her long red hair pulled to the side in a low ponytail over her shoulder. Her shoulders were bare, and her fair skin displayed a smattering of freckles. I used to tease her about them while kissing each one of them, which always made her laugh.

The pale blue of her tank top matched her eyes, making

them shine even brighter as she looked at me. There was a slight warning in them, but there was also trust. She was trusting me to enter Franny's life, but I could see that the mother in her was a protector. Again, something we had never had in a parent. I loved that she made sure our daughter had what we had always longed for. I would make sure that Franny got that from both parents now.

"Hello, Captain," Addy said, with a small smile. "Franny probably has a lot of questions for you. I hope you're prepared for an inquisitive little girl. But let's get some ice cream first and just get to know each other. Ease into this." She was in control, and I was OK with that. She knew what made Franny comfortable. Even if I wanted to stare at Franny and ask her about school and her favorite music and what kind of movies she liked, it wasn't time just yet.

I nodded my agreement and tried to reassure her with my gaze that I wouldn't mess this up. I wanted to keep that trust she'd given me. I wanted Franny happy, too.

We walked inside, and Franny looked up at her mom. "What kind are you getting?"

"Mint chocolate chip," I answered for Addy, remembering that she always chose it if it was available. I would sneak money from my mom's purse and take her to get ice cream after school whenever I could.

Addy's eyes widened, and she looked up at me before turning back to Franny. "Um, mint chocolate chip," she repeated.

Franny beamed at both of us. "She always gets that. I keep thinking she'll change her mind. She never does," Franny explained, as she looked over the different flavors.

"And you never get the same flavor twice," Addy said, then

took a quick peek at me. "Like someone else I know," she whispered, smiling. She was not only letting me know that she remembered that I liked to try every flavor but also showing me that our daughter had some of my traits, too. Franny might have been Addy's Mini Me, but she had her own personality. I could tell that already.

"I want to do the praline pecan. It has pecan pieces in it. See?" Franny said, pointing to the ice cream.

"Cone preference?" I asked her.

She turned her excited face toward me. "I like waffle cones."

I already knew what Addy liked. I turned to the young boy waiting to take our orders. "Two scoops of pecan praline in a waffle cone, two scoops of mint chocolate chip in a sugar cone, and a scoop of each of those in a waffle cone."

"Mommy never gets us two scoops," Franny said, her eyes big as she looked at her mother.

"It's OK. Today's a treat day," Addy assured her.

I felt Addy's gaze on me and met it with my own.

"You don't like mint chocolate chip," she said matter-of-factly.

That had been true at one point, but over the past ten years, mint chocolate chip was all I ever ate. I wasn't telling her that, though. Instead, I shrugged. "I'm a daredevil."

She grinned and shook her head, before reaching for the cone full of pecan praline that the guy handed over the counter. "Here you go, sweetie. Let's find a good spot in the shade to eat this."

Franny hurried for the door while licking her ice cream, and Addy turned back to me. "I'll pay for ours."

Like fucking hell she'd pay. "I got this," I said, then took her cone from the guy and handed it to her. "Go help Franny find a spot."

Addy studied me a moment, gave me a small nod, and did as I'd asked.

Addy

He was different. This wasn't the man I'd come to know over the past month. He wasn't as hard and cold. The fact that he remembered my favorite ice cream may have gotten to me a little. It was as if, for a moment, I had River again. I didn't want to expect that or hope for it, though. But I was glad for Franny that this was the man she would meet and know.

"He's really tall," Franny said quietly. "He seems strong."

Tall and strong. That was what she thought so far. I smiled as we sat down at a round table with a large umbrella blocking the sun.

"He also bought our ice cream. That's nice."

I agreed with a nod. "He's a good man." Deep down, I knew he was.

Franny grinned and licked her cone.

"Good spot," Captain said, as he pulled out a chair on the other side of Franny and across from me. "Ice cream good?" he asked, looking at Franny.

She wiped her mouth with the back of her hand while nodding vigorously. "I love it here. We got to come here once for a treat when we first moved in. But it costs a lot, so we don't come anymore."

I wanted to crawl under the table and hide, but I had nothing to be ashamed of. Franny was not a deprived child. She had a good life, and I'd given that to her. I held my head high, as if what she'd just said wasn't embarrassing to me at all.

"Ice cream all the time takes away the thrill of it. You'd get bored. Keeps it a treat when you only get it every once in a while," Captain said. I could feel his gaze on me, and I lifted my eyes from my own cone. He gave me a small smile and took a lick of his ice cream.

"Mom said that you used to take her to get ice cream a lot. Did it get boring?" Franny asked with complete sincerity.

Over the years, whenever she asked about her dad, she'd ask me to tell her something about him. She remembered every single story. I dropped my eyes back to my ice cream. I hoped he understood that I didn't fill her head because I was holding out hope that something would happen between us; I just gave her pieces of him along the way.

"Yeah, I did, and you have a point. It never got boring," Captain replied.

"I didn't think so. It tastes too good. We have ice cream for lunch at school on Wednesdays. But it doesn't taste like this, and it's only vanilla or chocolate."

"Is that so?" Captain was listening to her intently, and she was eating up the attention.

"Then on Fridays, we get a cupcake to celebrate all the birthdays that week, and sometimes we get red velvet. Those are my favorite. Except my friend Anna likes the chocolate ones best, so her favorite week isn't my favorite week and . . ." Franny had her father's attention, and she was on a roll. I leaned back and enjoyed my ice cream, while our daughter told Captain everything he could ever want to know about her life. She hardly came up for air. The only breaks he got were when she needed to take a lick of ice cream, and even then, he barely had a chance to catch his breath before she started talking again.

I stared out over the ocean, but every once in a while, I'd steal peeks at Captain to see how he was handling such a chatty nine-year-old. Every time, he looked fascinated. As if there was nothing she could say that would bore him. He nodded his head and said the right things at the right moments. This only made Franny more eager. I had a feeling she'd been saving it all up for this very day.

The way he interacted with her made it clear I'd been wrong to hold back from telling him about her. Hiding from him had been my way of protecting her, but had I really thought that the heart I once knew could be so different ten years later? Even if he had changed and hardened some, his goodness and protective instinct were still in there. I knew Franny had just become one of the luckiest little girls in the world.

Because when River Joshua Kipling decided you were worth protecting, he did it with everything he had.

Ten years ago

She was yelling, and we could hear her outside. River stopped at the front door and put his hand in front of me, holding me back. "You go to our spot at the pond. I'll deal with her and then meet you there."

If I didn't go into that house, she'd be furious. He knew that. Last week, she had thrown a glass at his head when he sent me to my room and told me to lock the door. I wasn't letting her do that again. Thank goodness his reflexes kept him from getting hit.

"No, I'm going in. She's been threatening for weeks to send me away. I don't want to give her a reason." I knew that using my fear of leaving him would be the only way he would agree.

"I won't let her."

"River, you can't stop her."

"She won't send you away, because she knows I'll report her. I'll call social services. I'll leave, too. She knows it. You're not going to be taken away from me." The determination in his voice made me feel safe, even though I was standing outside a house with a madwoman raging inside.

"She's on the phone with Dad," he said, reaching down to squeeze my hand. "Go to the pond for me."

I shook my head. "No. I won't leave you here."

River sighed, then turned to face me and placed both of his hands on my shoulders. He towered over me now at six feet. "Addy, please. I can handle her and calm her down. But if she hurts you, I will hurt her. I don't want to hurt my mother. She needs help. I need to go in there knowing you're safe."

I stared up at him, wishing he wasn't right. "I hate you having to deal with her alone. I hate being the reason."

He pulled me close to him and lowered his mouth to my ear. "You're my reason for everything." Then he kissed me on the cheek and straightened back up.

In the midst of this insane moment, I had butterflies in my stomach going crazy. But he always had that effect on me. "I can't remember what my life was like before you," I told him honestly. "And I don't want to remember."

He smirked. "I remember what mine was like before you, and I don't ever want to live without you again."

Captain

After our ice-cream date, Addy agreed to bring Franny over for dinner in three days on her night off. I was trying to give them both time to adjust to having me in their lives, but I sure as hell didn't want to wait that long. Watching Franny talk was fascinating. She was a ball of energy, and I felt like I had a lifetime to make up for with her.

The paperwork on my desk was waiting for me, but my head wasn't on work. It was on the two girls in my life. The only two I would ever love.

A knock interrupted my thoughts. "Come in," I called out.

Brad opened the door and stepped inside. I'd left a message for him to come see me. I had something we needed to discuss, and the kitchen wasn't the place to do it.

"Hey, you need me?" he asked, looking like he'd just crawled out of bed.

"Late night?" I asked, hoping he'd say yes. I wanted his attention off of Addy.

He nodded. "Yeah, I was up late trying a new idea for a menu. Took me three tries, but I think I nailed it. I'll make it today and let you try." The guy was obsessed with food, but that was what made him the best.

"You do that," I replied. "Close the door, and have a seat."

Today the new manager was coming into the restaurant, which was going to give me more time to spend with Franny—and her mother. Because I intended to spend time with Addy. Even if she seemed unsure about me.

"Brad, what's your relationship with Ad—I mean, Rose?" I corrected myself quickly. Calling her Rose was hard now. Remembering at work would be difficult. Explaining a name change to everyone wouldn't be easy.

Brad frowned and shifted in his seat. "Nothing yet. I mean, I think we're friends. I like spending time with her. Is that against policy? I assumed since you dated Elle, it was OK."

He went from nervous to defensive fast. "No, it isn't against policy, but I'm going to ask you to step back in your pursuit of Rose."

His frown deepened. "Why?"

Because she was my Addy, and I didn't want him fucking near her and making her laugh. "Because you have a kitchen to make first-class. Flirting with the servers isn't something you have time for. Rose has a daughter. She needs to focus on that when she's not here. So back off."

Brad stared at me a moment, then moved to stand up. "Not sure how me being her friend and seeing her after hours affects any of that. She's the best server we have, and you know it. She doesn't let anything affect that."

He needed to back down. My hands clenched tightly as I glared at him. "Don't push me on this," I said, lowering my voice to meet his challenge.

"Do you like her? Is that what this is about? Because last

time I checked, she isn't your speed. You go for the Elles of the world. And Rose isn't like Elle. Not even close."

I agreed with him completely on that. "I'm watching out for her. That's all. You can leave now." I didn't want to leave any room for argument.

He looked like he wanted to say more, but he didn't. I knew how I looked to him right now. He wasn't going to say anything with the warning in my glare. With a frustrated expression, he turned and left my office.

That had gone as expected, but it had to be done. Brad was the best chef around here, and I'd hate to fire him because he couldn't back off from Addy.

I got lost for the next few hours in paperwork and phone calls. When Jamieson Tynes finally showed up, I was annoyed and relieved. Arthur had said he'd be coming today, and I needed him here now more than ever. He would be my way to create the free time I needed for my daughter.

Leaving Rosemary Beach was no longer the plan. I'd come to terms with that immediately. Time with Franny and Addy was my top priority. I wanted to introduce them to my sister and bring them into my world. But Addy needed more first. She wasn't the same trusting girl who'd looked to me for everything.

My chest ached at the thought. I wanted that back. I wanted her looking at me as if she knew I'd make it all better. I knew she was strong. God, she'd proven that already with the way she had survived and raised our daughter. She was so much stronger than I realized.

But I didn't want her to have to be so fucking strong. I wanted to be there to give her someone to lean on. To share life with. My feelings for her had never changed. Even when I'd thought she was dead, she'd controlled me. She was the only reason I held on to the sliver of soul I had left. I wanted to keep some part of me for her. Even if she wasn't here.

"Are you Captain?" Jamieson asked, and I realized I'd gotten lost in my thoughts of Addy.

I stood up and held out my hand. "Yeah, that's me. I assume you're Jamieson."

He shook my hand and nodded. "Sorry I'm late. My flight from Dallas was delayed."

Just so, he was here. "No worries. I had stuff that I needed to straighten out this morning. I'll spend the rest of the day showing you the place and introducing you to the employees."

Jamieson was younger than me, but he had that fresh-out-of-business-school look about him, with his slacks and Oxford shirt. I knew he was taking in my faded jeans and black T-shirt. Sure, I always changed clothes before dinner service began, but during the day, I was comfortable. He'd need to learn to relax a little, too.

"Great. I'm excited about this opportunity."

I refrained from rolling my eyes. He was a kid. He'd lose that enthusiasm soon enough. He was about to enter the real world.

I walked past him and opened the door. "We'll start in the kitchen, and I'll show you around the back side of things. Introduce you to the culinary staff. We'll meet with the servers when they arrive in an hour."

Jamieson pulled an iPad Mini out of his briefcase. What the hell was he doing? "Can I leave my bag here?" he asked.

I just nodded, still trying to figure out what the iPad was for.

"Great. I'm ready to take diligent notes," he explained, holding up the iPad.

This was going to be interesting.

Addy

Franny had begged to come to work with me tonight. She wanted to hang out in the back with Captain. She didn't un-derstand that he was busy all evening, and he couldn't have her tagging along. But from the moment we had gotten back to the car after ice cream, she had talked nonstop about her fa-ther. She didn't call him Captain anymore, either. She referred to him as her dad when she talked about him to me. I knew she liked the way it sounded, but I worried that she was rush-ing things.

They both needed to ease into this.

Or maybe I needed them to ease into it. Maybe it was just me who needed space and time to adjust. Franny had been mine alone for so long. Sharing her like this—her emotions, her love—was hard. I hadn't expected that. I wanted her to have everything. I wanted her to know her father. I just didn't want her ever to feel like I hadn't been enough. That was my insecurity, though, and I knew it.

"Meeting in the dining room. The manager Captain's train-ing to take over is here. I hear he's young and super hot," Patri-cia informed me, as I went to stow my purse in the employee lounge.

"OK," I replied.

I knew Captain wasn't planning on staying. Everyone knew that. He hadn't kept that from everyone. But I hoped he wasn't leaving town. Not soon. Not now that I'd brought him into Franny's life.

"Dining room, now. Everyone," Elle called out in a bossy tone as she stepped into the room. Her gaze leveled on me, then she spun around and stalked off.

"Who wants to bet she fucks around with this one before the end of the week?" Daniel, one of the servers I didn't know well, whispered. Several of the others giggled quietly and muffled their laughter.

I really hoped she would, but that was a selfish hope I wasn't going to explore. I didn't need to think about it.

"You're not wearing your glasses," Natalie Orchard said, smiling at me. "I knew something was different about you. I like you in contacts. Your eyes are killer awesome."

There was no reason for me to wear the fake glasses now. I didn't explain that I didn't wear contacts. Instead, I just thanked her and followed everyone to the dining room.

I was unable to keep myself from scanning the room for Captain, and my eyes landed on him, then quickly looked away. I didn't want him to catch me looking at him. I was still confused about my feelings for him. When he was with Franny, I saw River in his expression. The hardness melted away, and the smile that used to make all the bad things in my life OK would touch his lips, and I would feel a tug I didn't want to feel. I wasn't ready to feel. I was afraid to feel.

"He's yummy," a female server whispered.

"He's all college-sexy," another said behind her hand.

"Dammit. He's straight. I can tell from here," Kyle muttered under his breath. That got me smiling. Kyle had been lusting after Captain from afar since the first day. He was open about how attractive he thought Captain was and how Captain's dangerous vibe made him sweaty and achy. That was more than I'd wanted to hear.

"No, he's definitely into girls. He's already checking Elle out," Natalie grumbled.

"Because she's flirting with him," Daniel replied. "She's either trying to make Captain jealous or mark her territory."

"Captain's not even paying attention. He's looking this way," Kyle said in a whisper. Then he turned to look at me and glanced back at Captain. "Or he's looking at Rose. You do look dayum good without glasses."

I smiled at Kyle. "Thank you."

He swung his gaze back to the front of the room and nodded. "Yep. He's checking out Rose."

I didn't want to look, but I was curious. Slowly, I turned my gaze to his, and our eyes locked immediately. He was watching me closely. A small smile tugged at the corners of his mouth, and I couldn't keep myself from smiling back.

"That shit's hot," Kyle drawled, and I jerked my gaze away from Captain and stared at my feet. Kyle chuckled, and Natalie let out a low whistle.

"Wowee. Someone caught the bad boy's attention. He's scary and hot all at the same time," Kyle said.

I ignored that. They didn't know Captain. They didn't know the boy he was or the life he had endured. But I didn't know what he'd lived through over the past ten years. Maybe the dangerous vibe they all got was real. An image of him laughing with Franny over a story she told him came back to me, and I shook the thought away. He wasn't dangerous. They just thought his slightly too long, sun-streaked hair pulled back in a man bun and the thick scruff on his face made him *look* dangerous. But I liked that scruff. I liked it a lot. It made me think about things. Things I hadn't had in a very long time.

"Someone's face is bright red. What did I miss?" Hillary asked as she stepped up beside me.

"Oh, just boss man up there, checking Rose out," Kyle supplied.

"How do you know he's not checking *me* out?" Hillary asked in a haughty tone.

"Because you just got here, and he's been zeroed in on that one since she walked into the room," Natalie replied, clearly enjoying herself. There was friction between them that I hadn't noticed before.

"Well, short stuff needs to get in line. He's mine next. Elle is moving to the new guy, it seems, and I want some of that badass up there. He'll look elsewhere once I get him alone for five minutes," Hillary said, then brushed past us with a sway in her hips, straight for Captain.

"She's a bitch," Natalie said in a disgusted tone.

"Most women are," Kyle said, then winked our way. "Present company excluded."

I wanted to continue to look at the floor or out the window. Anywhere but where my gaze was determined to go. I had to watch. I wasn't sure why. So what if she flirted with him and he liked it? He was my daughter's father. He was my past. I had no claim on him. But when she leaned in to whisper in his ear and his attention shifted from me to her, my heart cracked just a little. I couldn't help it. Old habits die hard.

"God, I hope he's smarter than that," Natalie muttered.

"Oh, he'll fuck her. His kind always takes the hot, easy fucks. They just don't commit. That's part of the sexy bad-boy thing that makes us all crazy," Kyle said.

"That's a shame," Natalie whispered, sounding as let down as I felt.

Captain lowered his head and responded to Hillary, while she kept a flirty, pleased smile on her face. What were they doing? Making plans for later? My gut twisted, and I hated it. I hated it so bad.

"You're dating Brad, aren't you?" Daniel asked. I looked at him and hoped the inner turmoil I was experiencing wasn't showing on my face.

"No, not really. We're friends is all," I corrected him. Brad flirted, but he didn't do more than that. He didn't call me or text me. We only talked at work, and he was a great guy, but I didn't want more from him. I liked the easy friendship we had fallen into.

"Ah, he just looks at you a lot, so I figured there was something more there," Daniel explained.

I didn't say anything to that. I was unaware that Brad looked at me a lot. I rarely looked in his direction unless we were talking.

Captain cleared his throat to get the room's attention. "OK, everyone. We're all here, so it's time to introduce you to your soon-to-be manager. Jamieson Tynes has been sent by Arthur Stout to take over in the next few weeks. While he's here, you're to make yourselves available for any questions. I'll start taking off a few nights a week and letting Jamieson take over, so the decisions and orders will be coming from him. Jamieson, I'm going to let you take it from here. This is your serving staff. Get to know them."

I looked at Jamieson, wondering if this bunch would eat him alive. He looked really young and naive.

"Oh, shit, here he comes," Kyle whispered. I looked up and saw the group of servers part like the Red Sea.

Captain.

"He's so determined. Sexy." Kyle made a strange pleased sound under his breath.

I couldn't look away this time. I watched wide-eyed as Captain came for me. There was a gleam in his eyes that excited me, but I wasn't sure what it meant.

"Rose, come with me," he said, loudly enough for the others to hear, although it was a soft demand.

I just nodded and followed him to his office. I was afraid to look at anyone else, but I could feel their eyes glued on us. Waiting to see what was going on.

I followed him obediently, because honestly, I wasn't sure anyone had ever told that man no. When had he learned to pack so much power into just one intent gaze and a few words?

When his office door opened, I went in right behind him, wondering if it was a mistake. He was in a strange mood, and I didn't know how I was connected to it. When I stepped inside, he closed the door, and I jumped a little at the loud *click*.

"You wouldn't look at me," he said in a tight, thick voice.

I *had* looked at him. Did he miss that? We were looking right at each other before Hillary came into the room. "I don't know what you mean," I said, slightly breathless from the intense atmosphere in the room.

"No, you were looking at me, and then you stopped and wouldn't look at me again."

How was he making the oxygen in the room so thin? I tried to take a deep breath. "I looked away when you did," I said in a whisper.

Captain took a step toward me, and the rest of the oxygen in the room evaporated. I needed to hold on to something. This wasn't a mood I'd seen him in before. I had no idea how to deal with it. "I don't want her. She offered. I sent her away. But you wouldn't look at me," he said, his voice so deep and raspy that I couldn't keep my chest from rising and falling with each short intake of air.

"Oh," I choked out, watching the storm in his eyes. The green had darkened to hazel, and the hard line of his mouth eased into something more . . . seductive. My legs felt weak.

"Yeah. Oh," he repeated. "Why didn't you look at me?"

Because I didn't like it. I had no reason not to like it, but I didn't. "I don't know," I lied.

The sharp upturn of the corners of his mouth told me he didn't believe me. But the fullness of those lips was fascinating. I could watch them up close like this all day and never get bored. Had they been that full all those years ago? Or had I been too young to appreciate the beauty of his mouth?

"Addy." His voice had gone even deeper, and I shivered at the sound of my name coming from those lips. He growled a curse that snapped my attention off his lips.

Looking at his eyes wasn't easier. They were dark now, his

pupils big with the intensity of his stare. "Don't lie to me. Why didn't you look at me?"

I blinked, trying to break this spell he was putting me under, but it didn't help. I was going to need to grab his arms to keep myself upright if he kept this up. That, or find a seat to sink into. "You stopped looking at *me*."

I forced myself to take a step back, hoping to get hold of myself, but Captain's move mirrored mine as he took a step with me. I felt like I was being caged in, and as much as that should have terrified me, it didn't. My head knew this was River. I couldn't be scared of him. We had too much between us.

"For a moment. I had to make myself clear to the girl. My eyes went right back where I wanted them, but . . ." He paused, and his hand moved to brush his knuckles along the outside of my arm so softly it was like a whisper. "You wouldn't look at me. I couldn't concentrate. I'm not even sure what all I said to the staff. I just wanted your eyes on me. I didn't like seeing you look at the floor. I wanted you to look at me."

Oh my. OK. This wasn't the man I was used to. This was not the man at the ice cream shop. Who the hell was this? And why was he making my heart beat so fast it was in danger of breaking through my chest at any moment? "I wasn't expecting this," I said, finally able to say something that made sense, that told him what I was feeling.

His gaze dropped to my mouth this time, and my knees buckled slightly. He looked hungry. Like he wanted to taste me. No, like he wanted me to be his last meal.

His large hands grabbed my waist. His touch was electric; I could feel the heat on my skin, even through my clothes. I might as well have been standing there naked.

"When I first saw you again, as Rose, I was unable to look away. No one had drawn me in like that. Not since . . . you. I didn't like looking at you because you moved like my Addy. You laughed like my Addy. You were petite and feminine, so much like my Addy, and I didn't want anyone around who reminded me of what I'd lost. I stayed away from anyone who reminded me of you in the slightest. But you were hard to ignore. I watched you more than I should have. I hated that you were calling to something inside me that I had reserved for one person. And then I find out that you *are* that person? You're here, and it's fucking with my head, Addy."

This was honesty. The kind of emotional honesty I hadn't expected. I'd known who he was all along; he had been the one in the dark, yet he had sensed me. It was *me* he was drawn to, no matter how I presented myself.

"There was Elle," I said simply, reminding myself as much as him. He might have sensed me, but it was Elle he had bent over his desk, in this very office.

His eyes clouded with regret. "She was a distraction. They've all been a distraction. There've been hundreds— I won't lie to you. But I didn't care for a single one of them. I never let them have me the way you had me. No one touched my soul, Addy. Only you."

My skin heated at his words. I hadn't slept with anyone since him. It had been ten years, and it was hard to believe, but I never wanted to be with anyone else. And until I loved again, I wasn't giving that part of myself to someone. Being intimate with someone brought them into my life, and that meant Franny's life. No one had ever been good enough.

"Hundreds?" I repeated. I wished it didn't hurt. But he

had thought I was dead. Would hearing him say he'd been in love with just one or two women be easier? No. It would have killed me.

"Never cared for them. Never saw their faces. Not one. I couldn't see anyone past you," he repeated, as he moved a hand up to cup the side of my face.

He needed to know. I wasn't ready for this. "I haven't been with anyone else . . . just you."

His hand tightened on my waist, and his body tensed. For a second, he closed his eyes and let out a deep sigh of what I knew was relief. Then his eyes were on me again, and his pupils were completely dilated. "No one?" he said, as if he was holding on to those two words as some sort of lifeline.

"No one," I repeated, because he seemed to need to hear it.

"Fuck," he whispered, and then he was gone.

I stumbled back, grabbing the back of a chair to keep myself steady. Captain turned and walked to his desk. He placed both palms on the top of it and hung his head as he stood there, looking like he was in some sort of turmoil.

I didn't say anything. I'd thought he'd want to know. That he'd want to hear he'd been it for me. But his reaction was confusing. I was finally able to take a deep breath; he was far enough away that his energy and presence didn't suck up all the air around me.

My head began to clear, and the spell he'd wrapped me in began to fade as he battled with himself.

"I'm not the same. I'm darker, Addy. I've done things that have broken me. The boy who worshipped you and treated you with care is gone. I don't know him anymore. He's not me. I'm . . . intense. Even with you, especially with you, I'd lose myself, and . . ." He shook his head, stood up, and turned to me. "What I want, what I like, it's not something you know. I can't go there with you."

Was he talking about sex? I was lost. "Why?" I asked, hoping he would make more sense.

He gazed at me with that look. A look I hadn't seen in so long that it hit me hard. That was the look I wanted. "You're too special, too fucking precious, for what I've become."

I didn't like that answer. I also didn't believe him. Just moments ago, he was looking at me like he wanted nothing more than to have me. "What if I want what you've become? What if the man I see is the one I want? Do I not get a choice?" I realized that I meant every word. I did want the man he had become. He was different, but so was I. Didn't he see that? I was harder and tougher, and I could survive. Just like him. It didn't make him less appealing. I was a woman now. I needed a man. Not the boy from my memories.

"You don't understand, and I can't tell you. If I did, you'd leave town and never look back. I can't let that happen. I want to prove that I can be the father Franny deserves. I won't let you down."

But he didn't want to be anything to *me*. It went unspoken, but it was clear. The realization sliced through me in a way that I'd never get over, but I *was* tough. I *was* a survivor, and I wouldn't beg anyone to want me. I'd done that as a child once, and my mother had left me anyway. Never again. Not even for River Joshua Kipling.

Captain

My mood had gone to hell. I'd snarled answers to anyone brave enough to ask, and Jamieson was annoying the shit out of me, in his suit, with his iPad Mini. Tonight couldn't end soon enough. Staying busy was all that kept me from stalking Addy and watching every move she made.

When she'd walked out of my office without a word, I'd known I'd been close to drawing her in. I could have kissed her. She'd have let me. When she had leaned into me and her body had responded to my hands, I'd felt like the king of the world. Then she'd told me what I'd already feared. The innocence that shone through her eyes wasn't an act.

While I had changed over the years, making sure to destroy my emotions to kill the pain, Addy had essentially stayed the same. She had become tough, and she'd learned to survive, but that only made her more special. How could I touch her? How was I even worthy to be near her? Fuck, if she knew the things I wanted to do to her, she'd be terrified. All she'd had was a boy who was so in love with her that sweet, easy sex had been perfect.

But I didn't want that with her. I wanted her naked and bent over my desk with her legs spread, so I could kneel between them and taste her, something I'd never done. I wanted her knees to buckle as I held her up with my hands and ran my tongue through her heat until she cried out my name, trembling from my kiss. Then I wanted to slam into her hard from behind and watch her face in a mirror as she came all over my dick. Because there would be no condom with her. I wanted nothing between us.

Closing my eyes, I considered leaving early. I couldn't keep this up. Every move she made, I knew it. Even if I wasn't watching her like I wanted to, I felt her. I knew who she was talking to and what she was doing.

Her laughter rang out, and my eyes snapped open, and a thick tightness rolled over me. She was in the kitchen. Motherfucker was making her laugh. The fury boiling in my veins was more than I could tamp down. He'd been warned.

I slammed through the back kitchen door, and my gaze locked on Addy immediately as she looked over at Brad. The smile was still on her face, and all I wanted to do was beat the hell out of my head chef until I had blood on my knuckles. The blackness I knew should never touch her cloaked me, and I couldn't stop. I kept moving toward them. This was the monster I didn't want her to see. The one I had lost control over.

"Don't," I said, my glare leveled on Brad. I didn't say more. The need to hurt him was choking me.

His eyes went wide, and I could see the uncertainty and fear. I wanted that. He needed to fucking fear me. I wasn't a whole man. I was a broken, fucked-up one, and he was getting too close to the one woman who owned me.

"Captain!" Addy's voice snapped at me, but I didn't look at her.

I kept my eyes locked on Brad until he nodded and dropped his attention to the food in front of him.

"Captain," Addy said again, clearly annoyed.

I turned to look over her head at the wall. I couldn't let her see my eyes right now. I knew the evil she'd see there. The evil that seeped through me.

"This isn't OK." She sounded furious now.

"Don't let him near you" was all I said, before walking away.

If she didn't understand why I'd done what I'd done earlier today, then I wasn't sure she would ever get it. I had to go outside and calm down. There wasn't a gym open at this time in this small town, and right now, I needed to hit something until I was too exhausted to stand up.

"Table five is unhappy with their steak, although it's cooked to their requested temperature," Jamieson said, hurrying toward me.

I didn't give a rat's ass if table five was unhappy. "Handle it. No time like the present to learn to deal with shit," I said, with a snarl I couldn't control, before heading outside.

Ten years ago

When I opened the door to Addy's room, I froze. My breathing ceased. My heart stopped. I couldn't move. It was late, and my mother was asleep across the house near my own bedroom. I had been waiting until I knew her sleeping medicine had kicked in before coming to Addy.

This wasn't what I was expecting. In her dark room, with the moonlight shining down on her, Addy stood in front of me wearing nothing. Absolutely nothing. I needed to speak or breathe or something, but I couldn't take my eyes off of her. I was afraid I was asleep, and if I moved, I'd wake up, and this would be gone.

I'd thought about her like this. I knew she'd be beautiful, but never did I realize just how perfect she would be. She shivered, and that was enough to wake me from my trance so that I could at least get the door closed and locked. She was naked, and it wasn't an accident.

"Hey," she said softly, and my dick, which was already at attention, jerked. What was she doing?

"Hey," I croaked, my eyes on her creamy, plump breasts, completely bared to me.

My eyes lowered to take in her flat stomach and the freckle just beside her belly button that I loved. Then I sucked in a breath as I lowered my gaze to see the small triangle of blond hair.

"Addy," I whispered, as she continued to stand like that for me.

"Yes?" She sounded as affected by this as I was.

"You're beautiful . . . perfect," I said, in awe.

"I am?" She sounded unsure but hopeful.

God, had she never looked in the mirror? This was . . . shit, this was every fantasy I'd ever had. "Completely," I assured her, tearing my eyes off her body to look at her face. She smiled shyly. "What's going on, Addy?" I was afraid to hope.

"I want to . . . tonight. I'm ready."

Fuck. OK. We'd been messing around a little at night while kissing, but I always ended it before it got painful. This was not what I expected from her. "Why? I mean, are you sure?" My eyes drifted back over her smooth skin that I so wanted to touch. That I wanted to feel move against mine.

"Because I love you, and I want to be as close to you as I can be," she whispered.

I made a step toward her, and my hands trembled as I got closer. This was it. Tonight I'd have her in a way no one else ever would. She would become mine completely. We would know each other more deeply. Our connection was already unlike anything I'd ever experienced in my life, but this would make it unbreakable.

"Are you sure?" I asked, before I reached out to touch her bare hip.

"Yes," she said, and I didn't hesitate. I pulled her to me and claimed her mouth, while her body molded to mine. The sex I'd had in the backs of cars and other less appealing locations had been for release, because I was horny and they were willing and it felt good.

But this was different. I wanted to memorize every second. Every inch of her body. When I sank inside Addy, I would give her all of me that she didn't already own. "I love you so much," I said against her lips, as I moved us over to her bed.

"I love you, too," she said, gazing up at me with all the trust in the world.

I'd never been with a virgin. "It will hurt you at first," I told her, praying she wouldn't back out now.

She smiled and ducked her head against my chest. "I know, but with your arms around me, it won't matter. We'll be as close as we can get. That's what I want more than anything."

My trembling was getting worse. The excitement, need, and desire inside for this one girl, mixed with how much I loved her, was almost too much.

"Take off your shirt, River. I want to feel you against me with nothing between us," she said against my chest, then moved back just enough so I could do as she asked.

Her breasts moved up and down quickly as her breathing became more rapid. Her eyes were on my shirt, and I reached for it to pull it over my head. Her tight pink nipples teased me, and the idea of feeling them against my bare chest brought me dangerously close to coming in my jeans. This might be more than I could handle.

Dropping my shirt, I stared at her, waiting. I needed her to make the move. I was afraid of scaring her. Without hesitation, she lifted her arms to wrap around my neck as she stood on her tiptoes and pressed her breasts against me.

"Fuuuuck," I whispered in a groan, unable not to respond verbally.

"It feels so good, doesn't it?" she said with a soft moan.

"Yes," I replied, moving my hands down her back until they slowly cupped her bare butt. I lifted her up, pressing her against me, and then she wrapped her legs around me, putting her center right over my crotch. The heat from her seared through my jeans. The image of her being open like this and pressed against me just about made my knees buckle. I had to sink onto the bed, holding her.

She moved her hips slightly, and the heat in her eyes ignited. "Oh, that . . . oh," she said softly. She was moving her sensitive clit over the ridge in my jeans. I held her still.

"Don't, baby. This will be over before it begins if you do that. I can't handle it. I'm already too close," I told her, my voice low and gravelly.

"OK, well, can you get naked, then, too?"

The fact that she was turned on enough to ask me something so brave and out of character had me smiling. Addy was asking me to get naked. If I was asleep, I was going to wake up so fucking pissed.

Addy

Listening to Franny talk about our dinner date with Captain in two nights' time was hard. I wasn't ready to see him, much less have dinner with him. As a matter of fact, as soon as Franny left for school that morning, I was calling in sick. I didn't want to face him today. Not after the roller coaster last night.

I went from feeling like we were connecting to feeling totally rejected. I actually wanted him, but he had tossed me aside because I hadn't had sex in ten years. To make things even more brilliant, when Brad had joked that he'd put a corn cob up the ass of a particularly difficult guest, which was the only thing that had made me laugh that whole shitty day, Captain had come stalking into the kitchen like a madman. He was furious because Brad had made me laugh? Was that unacceptable?

"And I told Cameron how tall my dad is and that he has big muscles. He has big muscles, doesn't he, Mommy?"

Yes, her father had muscles. Not the body-builder kind but the tough working-man kind. I nodded and took a mouthful of my oatmeal. He also had really amazing eyes, and his lashes were long and dark compared with the highlights in his hair.

"She said her daddy was bigger, but I know he's not. Mine is more handsome. I know that. I don't think anyone has a daddy as handsome as mine."

She had a point there. I wasn't going to comment, though. I just kept spooning up my oatmeal.

"Do you think he'll be at my birthday party?"

Franny's birthday wasn't for another five months. I had no idea what the future held for us and Captain. I had never lied to her before. I'd been honest about everything. Except, of course, keeping the truth from her about the reason we were in Rosemary Beach, but that had been a temporary omission.

"I don't know, Franny. That's a long way off, and we're just now easing him into our lives. He could move away." I'd heard he'd never planned on sticking around here for long. "He could visit you when he has time. I just don't know right now."

The light in Franny's eyes dimmed some. I hated to be the cause of that, but how could I promise her something I wasn't sure of?

"If he can be there, then he will be. That I do know," I assured her, wanting to ease my too-blunt answer.

She smiled then. "I bet he'll want to be. You can make a big, yummy red velvet cake. I love those. He does, too—he said so. I asked him. He'll love yours. You make the best."

"If red velvet is what you want, then that's what I'll make," I assured her.

She seemed happy with this. Standing up, she walked over and kissed my cheek. "I'll brush my teeth, and then I'll be ready for school."

I nodded, gave her a squeeze, and watched my little girl

bounce off. I wanted her to have it all. And to her, Captain was part of that.

If only I could control everything in her life and fulfill all of her hopes and dreams.

Once Franny was at school and I was back home, I put on a pair of shorts and a tank top and decided it was a good time to clean the house from top to bottom. I was thankful it was Jamieson who answered when I called in sick. He told me he hoped I was better soon and was very professional and polite. I wondered how long his enthusiasm was going to last.

Not having to deal with Captain had been a major plus for me. I wasn't sure if this would affect my night off, though. I knew he wanted to eat with Franny. I figured since he was still the boss, he'd make sure I was still off work that night.

Today's plan was to clean and forget yesterday completely. Especially the moments in his office when I'd made a fool of myself by melting into him like an idiot. The way he had dismissed me so easily had felt like being doused with a bucket of cold water. After watching the way he'd treated women for the past month, I had thought I was smarter than that.

I didn't blame Elle now. If he'd turned that smoldering, breathtaking intensity on her, no wonder she was obsessed with him. And he hadn't turned her away, either. He'd taken what she was offering. My offering, however, was too inexperienced for him. Asshole. Womanizing asshole.

Once, I had been what he wanted. The fact I'd only been with him had made us closer. He'd been proud of it and made me feel special. Our eyes would lock across a crowded hallway at school, and we'd connect without words. It had bonded us in a way that ruined me for anyone else. I hadn't wanted that kind of connection with someone else.

That had changed for him, though. He wanted other things now, and he didn't want to teach me. Fine. Whatever. I didn't need him, either. The only thing I hated was that his actions were tarnishing the memory of what we once had. I'd held the memory of one particular night close, and it had kept me warm when I was lonely. Now it was not enough. Or maybe *I* simply wasn't enough.

Ten years ago

I stared at myself in the bathroom mirror. Could others see that I was different? I felt different, and I could see the difference.

River had held me for hours last night after we'd had sex. Then he'd cleaned me up and taken care of my sheets early this morning, before pulling me back into his arms for a kiss and going back to his room.

I hadn't been able to go back to sleep after he'd left. All I could do was smile as I stared at the ceiling, remembering every moment. It had hurt, but the way he had held me and whispered in my ear about how much he loved me had helped ease the throbbing until he could move again.

His face when he'd stilled and stared down at me, his jaw going slack and his eyes glazing over, had been beautiful. I wanted to see that again. Seeing the condom as he'd pulled it off, streaked with my blood, had startled me, but he'd taken his T-shirt and cleaned between my legs, telling me it was normal the first time. I trusted him. I didn't feel that saying I loved him was enough now. It was so much more than that. He was what completed me. He made my life full.

Now River came up behind me, slipped his arms around my waist, and looked at our reflection in the mirror. I watched him as he turned his head to kiss my temple before looking back at me. Our eyes said more than we ever could.

His tanned arms were turning into the muscular arms of a man, and I loved having them around me. I also loved the way they'd flexed as he'd held himself over me last night. For a moment, I'd been lost in the way the muscles moved with each rock of his hips. Another thing about him that was beautiful.

"How do you feel?" he asked me, watching me closely.

The smile on my face should have told him all he needed to know. "Perfect."

He swallowed hard and put his palm flat against my stomach and pulled me tighter against his chest. "Me, too."

Captain

Her car was in the driveway when I pulled up to Addy's house. When I'd gotten to the office and found out she'd called in sick, I had turned and walked right back out. She wasn't sick. At least, I hoped she wasn't. I was more than positive she'd called in sick to stay away from me. Which I deserved, dammit. Last night had gone wrong. I wanted to get close to her and have a relationship with my daughter.

I wanted Addy. There, I said it. I fucking wanted Addy. The idea of her with anyone else drove me mad. But how could I have her? The man I was now could never be someone she would love.

I parked my truck and headed for her door, not sure what I intended to say, but I had to say something. This thing between us had to be fixed for Franny's sake—and my sanity. Sleeping last night had been impossible. The look on Addy's face before she had turned and walked out of my office had taunted me. How could I protect her from me? I'd protected her from everyone else, but I'd never had to protect her from me.

The small porch of the guest house they rented was clean, with potted flowers giving the place a homey feel. Even the steps were swept clean. Addy gave our daughter so much. I'd never be able to give her what Addy could. But I wanted to give her everything in my power.

Before I hit the top step, the door swung open, and Addy stood there, glaring at me. That should have been the first thing I worried about: what I was going to say to fix this. But that wasn't what caught my attention.

She wasn't wearing a bra. Her much larger breasts were crammed into a top that wasn't quite big enough to contain them. God help me, I wanted her naked.

"Why are you here?" she snapped.

I had to shake my head and force my eyes off her tits to regain focus. Looking up at her angry face helped. I didn't want her angry at me. I had to find a way to make up for last night and the shitty way I'd handled things. But she needed a bra. A potato sack would be even better. "I came to talk," I said.

"Talk," she said, not moving from the door, a look of steel on her face. That only made her hotter. A mad Addy was not a scary one.

"Can I come in?"

"No," she snapped.

I was going to have to do better than this. "Addy, I'm sorry. I was an asshole last night, and I would like to talk about what happened. Please."

That softened her up a bit. I could see the anger she was using like a shield slip some. She bit down on her bottom lip and took a step back. That was a good sign. "OK. Fine."

When she turned to walk back inside, I took the moment to enjoy the view of her ass. It was a jerk move, but her body was so filled out now, and I hadn't seen it naked looking like this. The body I had once claimed as mine no longer looked the same, and I wanted to see more of it.

"Would you like a drink?" she asked, glancing back at me.

I jerked my gaze off her butt to shake my head. "No, I'm good, thanks."

"OK, then, talk." She looked at me with a directness I wasn't used to from her. Lately, she hardly looked me in the eyes. But then I'd brought that on myself, too. She motioned for me to take a seat on the sofa, and she sat in the chair across from it.

I wished I'd come more prepared. I had made a rushed decision to come over once she wasn't at work, but now that I had her alone, I didn't know where to start. She looked annoyed. Again, I wasn't used to that.

"What happened in my office, I handled that wrong. I got caught up in the moment, and then your words brought me back to reality. For . . ." I paused, because this next part needed to be worded carefully. Upsetting her now wasn't a good idea. I doubted she'd give me another chance to rectify things. And for Franny's sake more than anything else, I needed her to like me. Trust me. Again.

"The past ten years vanished, and it was just us. You were . . . mine, and I lost my head. I was back there in that time when you trusted me and you were the reason I woke up every morning. My head was slow catching up with my heart or emotions or whatever. I just handled it all wrong. When I realized what I was doing, it was too late. I'd taken a step too far."

Addy's gaze dropped to her lap as she twisted her hands.

I'd have given anything to know what she was thinking. I replayed what I'd said in my head, hoping it sounded the way I'd meant it to. Downplaying what had happened between us wasn't what I wanted to do. Not with Addy. Because I had been lost in her at that moment and wouldn't take it back.

"I think I got lost, too. You were just River for a moment. So I understand." She lifted her gaze to meet mine, and I saw hurt there that twisted my gut. "But what happened in the kitchen? Why did you get so angry? Neither Brad nor I did anything to ignite your anger."

Shit. Fuck. I didn't have an answer for this, and if this was why she looked hurt, I hated that even more. The idea that she might have feelings for Brad just about undid me. I couldn't handle it. No, we weren't the Addy and River from our past, but hell if I was going to sit back and let her fall in love with another man when I'd been the only one she'd ever known.

That knowledge had kept me up all night. Addy had only been touched by me. She'd given herself to me, and she was still mine in that sense. Whether she wanted to admit it or not, she had saved herself for me. In her heart, she belonged to me.

Fuck if that didn't make me feel like a caveman. I wanted that. I loved it. I obsessed over it. And I wanted to keep it that way. Fact was, I couldn't keep every Brad out of her life, nor did she deserve that. It wasn't fair.

Especially since I was too fucked-up to be what she needed.

I knew she was waiting for me to answer her. I could lie. It would be easier on both of us. But I didn't want to lie to her.

"I was jealous," I said simply. Her eyes widened, and she

didn't say anything, but the surprise on her face meant that I needed to say more. She'd get the wrong idea.

"You'd just told me I was the only man you'd ever been with. Old feelings came roaring back, and I won't lie to you, Addy, for a man, that's intense. Especially when we had the connection we had. One that has stayed with me and changed the course of my life. Knowing you'd only been with me, well, that had me raw. When I heard Brad making you laugh, I snapped. The possessiveness I have no right to feel clawed to the surface, and I acted like a jackass. I shouldn't have. I won't again. I'm sorry."

Addy let out a sigh and nodded. She kept her expression neutral. The only thing that gave anything away was her eyes. They were unsure. That much I knew. I wouldn't lead her on. I couldn't do that to her or our daughter. What we needed was a friendship. That was something I could give her. I'd keep the dirt on my hands off her.

"I want to be in Franny's life. She's perfect. I thought she was all you, but she's just your look-alike. She has me in her as well, and seeing that is the most precious gift I've ever been given. You were the only family that mattered in my life for so long. Now you've given me someone who's a part of me. Someone I can love unconditionally."

Addy's eyes filled with unshed tears, and she sniffed and nodded her head. "OK. Yeah. I want you in her life, too. She wants you there. She's already telling everyone at school her father is the biggest, strongest man on earth." She blinked back the tears. "Our past will come up sometimes. It's impossible for it not to. Emotions will get tangled, and I don't think we can stop that from happening. But I want Franny to have you in her life. I want her to have what we didn't."

Addy had already given her that, but I understood what she meant. I wanted that, too. I just had to protect Addy from me while giving them both what they needed.

Addy

Things at work went smoothly with Captain after he came over. I tried not to wish for more. Every time he smiled at me or made a joke, watching me to see if I'd laugh, my heart melted a little more. I knew that guy. River was beginning to show through, and every time he did, I fell just a little more.

Brad had taken a major step back, and I was actually relieved. I didn't want to feel like I had to be careful around Brad if he flirted with me. Captain had said he wouldn't do it again, but I simply didn't like the idea of Captain having a hard time watching Brad and me together. Maybe that was a weak-woman thing, and maybe I should be stronger. Make him suffer. But I didn't play games. I wasn't going to start now.

I wasn't interested in Brad romantically, so using him to get to Captain was wrong. Luckily, Brad had taken Captain's hint and backed off completely. Now he simply nodded when he saw me. I rarely even got a smile.

When that didn't sting, I knew that Brad had just been filling the emptiness I'd lived with for ten years. He deserved better than to be the filler guy. He was a great guy. Just not the one I wanted.

Tonight was our dinner night with Captain. Franny had

been bouncing off the walls since she'd gotten home from school. She had asked me three times if her sundress was pretty. It was her favorite sundress, and seeing her so eager to please Captain made me smile.

"Come here," I told her, drying off my hands after washing up the rest of the dishes from this morning.

She walked over to me, looking up at me with eyes so much like my own.

"Your father thinks you're the most beautiful, perfect little girl he's ever seen. He's proud of you. He'll love this dress, but he would also love the denim shorts and T-shirt you were wearing earlier. He doesn't care what you wear. His love is not something you have to earn. He loved you the moment he found out you were his. It's the way a good parent is. We love unconditionally, because we can't help it. You're ours."

Franny let out a sigh and smiled, looking like I had just taken a huge burden off her shoulders. "OK," she whispered. "That's good. Because I don't want him to leave."

That kind of fear was something I never wanted her to deal with. I was going to talk to Captain about it. I had been honest with her about not being able to control what happened with Captain. He could still leave Rosemary Beach, but I hoped he wouldn't. He needed to know Franny was struggling with it. Only Captain could ease her mind about this. Not me. She knew I'd always be here. We were a team. Captain hadn't made the team yet. She didn't trust him in that way. He had to earn that.

"Let's enjoy tonight. You'll have his complete attention," I told her, avoiding the rest of her comment.

Franny gave me a crooked grin that was her father's. I didn't point that out to her. "Not all of his attention," she said, then turned and flounced into the living room.

I didn't ask her what that meant. Her thoughts bounced all over the place.

"He's here!" she squealed, just as the tires from his truck crunched over the shell driveway. "He's early!" she added, running to the door.

He was ten minutes early. That would mean a lot to Franny. I waited where I was and let her open the door and greet him.

Captain's eyes immediately dropped to her as she swung the door open when he hit the top step.

"Hey," she said, in her bubbly tone that meant all was right with her world. Thanks to him.

Captain grinned, and the corners of his eyes crinkled, which was new for me. They were marks of a man. A man who had smiled over the years. He'd had reasons to smile. I was thankful for that. I didn't want to think of him as unhappy.

"Aren't you a pretty picture?" he said, and I seriously could have kissed him right then. He'd said exactly what she needed to hear. I also wanted to kiss him because, in that button-up blue shirt and faded jeans, he was a bit overwhelming. A man shouldn't be that beautiful. It wasn't fair.

"It's my favorite dress," she told him, and spun in a circle to show him how it flared a little at the bottom.

"I can see why," he replied, and she beamed even brighter.

When he lifted his gaze, it locked on me, and I wished my heart didn't beat a little faster. This was not what we needed. It was not what he wanted. It was a big mistake for me to be attracted to him. It was an even bigger mistake to feel things for him. He could destroy me.

"Like mother, like daughter," he said with a slow grin. "Ain't every day a man gets to take out two of the prettiest girls in town."

Franny giggled and turned to look back at me. I managed to get hold of myself and smile back. I walked over to the sideboard, where I had left my purse. With my back turned, I took a deep breath and gave myself a small pep talk in my head.

"All right, lucky man, let's go." I tried to sound teasing, but I was afraid my voice wavered a little.

Captain held out his hand to Franny, who instantly stuck her small hand in his and led him out the door. I wanted to stop walking and just watch them go. He was so big and masculine, and at times he seemed dangerous. But seeing him with Franny's little hand in his, her head tilted up, chatting away, was breathtaking.

I touched my stomach and ordered my ovaries to calm down before they combusted. *Get over it, Addy.*

Franny climbed into the front of Captain's truck and tried to scoot over so I could fit, too. But I needed the space to get myself together again. I opted to get into the back of his extended cab. Franny buckled up happily and began to tell Captain about every moment of her day.

I listened to him respond when he needed to, and it was obvious he was enjoying himself. I couldn't imagine him leaving Rosemary Beach. Not when he wanted this relationship. For Franny's sake, this was another conversation I'd have to have with him.

Deep down, I knew that I didn't want him to leave for self-ish reasons as well. Although Addy came first in all things, for the first time since I'd held her in my arms, I wanted something for me, too. Something I could never have, so I had to deal with it, and fast. Franny's happiness came first.

Captain

I couldn't get out of my truck fast enough. Chatting with Franny was incredible. She wanted to tell me everything, and I loved it. But God help me, Addy smelled so damn good my hands were sweating. Her scent had engulfed my truck, and every small move she made was like an electric jolt to my senses. I was so wound up by the time we parked that I jerked open my door and climbed out just to take a deep breath that wasn't filled with Addy.

Clearing my head was the most important thing right now. I was getting to know my daughter and building a friendship with her mother. Not getting a fucking hard-on every time I thought about Addy's soft skin was the most important thing right now.

Jesus, I was fucked.

I took one more breath of Addy-free air before walking around the front of the truck to open Franny's door and help her down. Addy opened her own door and climbed out. I'd wanted to help her, too, but she hadn't waited, so I let it go. She wanted to define this thing with us, and I had to let her.

I was caving fast. My good intentions were hard to hold on to when she smelled like heaven, looked like an angel, and was wearing a fucking red sundress. Damn dress was making it hard to keep my attention off her.

"What place is this?" Franny asked.

"It's the best burger place around, and it's on the water. I thought I'd take us out of Rosemary Beach for a change. This is Grayton Beach. You'll like it. There's live music outside on the water if you want to listen after we eat."

She smiled brightly and nodded. I was beginning to think she'd be happy to do whatever I suggested. That was a humbling realization. This little girl had just met me, and she already wanted to be near me, to talk to me, to have me in her life. This should have been harder, but with Franny, nothing was hard.

Now, with her mother . . . I shook that thought off. I wasn't thinking about Addy right now. I'd do that at home alone tonight.

"I can play the guitar," Franny announced, watching me closely. "Mommy taught me. But she plays better."

Unable not to look at Addy, who was walking quietly behind us, I let myself get lost for a moment, in a time when we were us, when she would only play for me. I remembered when I'd traded my baseball card collection that my dad had given me, which his dad had given him, for a used guitar at a pawn shop. Addy never knew how I got that guitar, and I never told her, but she'd loved it. We had kept it hidden under her bed, and she had only played it down by the pond or whenever my mother wasn't home. When she'd left—when I thought she was gone—I'd gotten the guitar from under her bed. It was in a box, stored safely in my boathouse. I hadn't taken it out in years.

Tonight I would. Holding it wouldn't cause unbearable pain now. When the time was right, I'd give it back to its rightful owner.

Addy shifted her gaze to meet mine, and a smile touched her lips. "She's a natural," she said.

I made myself look away from her. "I bet she is. Her mother is incredibly talented," I said, looking straight ahead so neither of the girls could see my eyes; they'd say more than needed to be said.

"Did Mommy play for you when you loved her?" Franny asked innocently.

When you loved her. Those four words were too much. I just nodded.

"She used to play for me at night and sing me songs until I fell asleep. Then she taught me to play," Franny continued.

Another thing Addy had given our daughter.

"Hey, they have homemade Key lime pie here!" Franny said, doing a little jump of happiness. "Look at that sign. It's the world's best. I love Key lime pie."

"Then we'll order a whole pie and eat until we're sick," I told her.

She giggled, then looked back at her mother. "I think he's teasing. I won't eat until I'm sick."

Addy's soft laugh sent warm tingles down my spine. "I'm sure he's teasing."

"Me? Teasing? I'm completely serious," I said, glancing back over my shoulder to wink at her.

The flash of heat in her eyes didn't go unnoticed.

Yeah. We were fucked. If she wanted me like I wanted her, we were so screwed.

Franny let go of my hand and ran up the steps to the door of the restaurant. I followed her and put our name in with the hostess. When I turned to find the girls, I saw Franny studying the large tank of saltwater fish. Addy was behind her, pointing out different fish and telling her what they were. The two of them were a lot to take in. I could see others looking at them. One guy from the bar was watching Addy with interest. I leveled a warning glare at him as I walked up behind them and placed my hand on Addy's lower back.

The man's gaze shifted to me and then dropped back to his drink. He got the message. I saw then that Addy was staring at me. She had gone very still.

It took me a moment to realize that my hand had made her tense. There was no way to get around the fact that I'd just touched her in a gesture of possession. As much as I didn't want to, I dropped my hand and looked at the tank. "I'm impressed your momma knows all the names of these fish."

Franny glanced back at me and grinned. "Mommy knows everything," she informed me with complete sincerity, then turned back to the fish tank.

I disagreed. If she knew everything, she'd know that dress she was wearing and the perfume she had on was driving me crazy. My touching her back like she was mine wouldn't have surprised her. If she knew everything, she'd know I was hanging on by a thread.

"Kipling, table for three," the hostess said behind me.

"That's us." I took Franny's hand.

"Yay!" Her small hand held mine tightly, and I kept it there as we followed the hostess to our table. I'd requested one by the window so we could have a view. Franny sat at the chair by the window and looked up at me hopefully. I knew where she wanted me. I took the seat beside her, and she beamed and looked back at the water outside.

Addy took the chair across from me. And I could smell her.

"Look, they're playing volleyball out there," Franny said, pointing to some kids on the beach.

I tried not to imagine things about Addy that I shouldn't be imagining and tried to focus on my daughter. This night might be the longest of my life, but I couldn't think of anywhere else I'd rather be.

Addy

By the time Captain pulled into our driveway, Franny had fallen asleep in the front seat. He parked and looked back at me with a small smile. "We wore her out."

"She wore herself out. I wish I had a fourth of her energy," I replied, opening my door. "But she enjoyed tonight. Thank you for making it special." I had the Key lime pie in my lap. Her eyes had lit up when it arrived at the table, and although she had barely finished one slice, it was important to her that he had bought the whole pie.

I climbed down just as Captain walked over to our side. He started to open her door but stopped and looked at me. "Did you have a good night?" His question was sincere. As if he wanted me to say yes.

I'd had a wonderful night, but there were times when I'd forgotten who we were and what we weren't. The lines had blurred again, and the fantasy that we were the happy family the server thought we were was easy to buy into. I couldn't let that become something Franny expected. "It was really nice. Thank you," I replied.

He tilted his head and studied me for a moment. "Just nice, huh?"

The fact that this man needed reassurance was sweet. I wanted to kiss that look off his face, but I quickly snapped out of my giddy moment and stepped back.

Captain followed me with a step of his own. Confused, I watched him, wondering what this was. I couldn't play teasing games with him.

"Don't," he said softly, when I started to move away again. "Just for a moment, let me be close to you. I know this isn't what you want. It isn't smart. But . . ." He closed his eyes tightly and clenched his teeth. "I just need to touch you."

Oh, God. Oh. God. I was frozen, and moving was impossible.

He moved in closer, until our chests almost touched. We'd been here before. It hadn't ended well. But although my head was screaming at me to stop, my heart was pounding, and the butterflies in my stomach had taken flight.

"All night, I've been drowning in your scent," he said in a husky whisper, and he lowered his head, his nose brushing my neck.

I let out a shaky breath as I listened to him inhale deeply. "Incredible. My whole truck smells like you now. I'm not going to be able to get you out of my head. Not that I could before."

His words made my brain go a little foggy. Not good. A hand touched my waist and ran down to settle on my hip.

"So good," he said, still running his nose along the sensitive skin of my neck. "Nothing's ever been this good."

I should have moved. I should have said something. Instead, I grabbed his biceps to steady myself. I was an idiot, but at the moment, I didn't care. I wanted more.

When his lips touched the base of my throat, I inhaled so sharply I startled myself and tightened my hold on him. "Just let me taste a little. I need a small taste of you. I swear, I'll stop." I wasn't sure if he was begging me or convincing himself.

If I could talk, I would tell him I was at his mercy, and he could do whatever he wanted. It had been so long since I'd been touched like this. So very long.

His other hand slid over my hip and then behind my back, until it was pressed against my bottom. He pulled me close as his lips trailed kisses along my collarbone and back up my neck.

My head fell back, giving him more access to my neck. My body was becoming liquid heat, and I was sure he could do whatever he wanted at this point, and I'd let him.

His other hand slid into my hair and cupped the back of my head while he kissed his way up my neck, stopping to give me small licks where my pulse beat furiously. He pressed his tongue against one small point and groaned.

"I need your mouth again, Addy," he said. Before I could even think to respond, he covered mine with his own.

I gave him what he wanted, because I wanted it, too. The plumpness of his lips drove me to shiver and cling desperately to him. He picked me up until our bodies were flush. The friction I'd get if I opened my legs and wrapped them around him was so tempting I had to fight not to do it. I had to stop this.

Franny was asleep in the truck, but if she woke up, she'd see us, and it would confuse her. She'd think something was happening that wasn't. Because this didn't change anything.

He'd said he wanted friendship. So why was I giving him this?

I tore my mouth from his and pushed him away. To get space. To clear my head. God, I was so weak. Franny could have woken up and seen this. What was I thinking? When had I gotten so careless? Furious with myself, I shoved the lingering need back. Franny came first.

"We can't do this," I said, sounding like I'd just run five miles.

The look in Captain's eyes was too much, so I looked over his shoulder at the moon. I couldn't look at him right now. I felt the heat he was feeling, too. I just didn't know what we were going to do with it. Because quickie grope sessions were not something I was OK with.

"I fought touching you all night, and I just . . ." He paused. "I lost control for a minute. I had to touch you and taste you again."

Well, he got props for being honest. I glanced back at the truck, glad that Franny was still sleeping. "I need to get her to bed. It's late," I said.

"I'll carry her in," Captain said, turning to open the truck door and retrieve our daughter.

I opened the front door. Deep breaths and the evening breeze helped to cool my flushed skin. I could feel Captain's eyes on me as he walked inside, but I wouldn't look at him. I couldn't. He had to know how this made me feel. This wasn't fair. He wasn't being fair.

"Where to?" he whispered. I nodded in the direction of the bedroom and led the way so I could pull back the covers.

I slipped off her sandals and quickly tucked her in, kissing her forehead as she curled deeper into the covers. When I turned around, Captain was watching her sleep. The love in his eyes made my stomach feel funny, and I had to leave him there. If he wanted to soak in that moment, fine. But I didn't have to watch him do it. That played with another set of my heartstrings.

I felt him move and knew he was following me. The soft *click* of the bedroom door made me wish I'd stayed in there with Franny. Safe from him. Safe from my weakness and emotions.

"I'm not going to apologize for that out there," he said, his voice low.

I didn't turn back to look at him. "I was a willing participant. No need for you to apologize."

He let out a heavy sigh. "Come on, Addy. Look at me."

The idea of looking at him scared me. Even now, my body was still humming. Looking at him would not help. "It's late," I said.

I heard his heavy footsteps and tensed as his warmth drew closer to me. If he touched me, I had to remember myself. Our daughter was asleep just a room away.

"I want to protect you. From everything. I always have. But I don't think I can protect you from me. I thought I could." His voice was so close I could feel the warmth of his breath. "I can't. I want you too bad. I want to be able to touch you. It's not gone for me, Addy. None of it is gone."

I took a step back and bumped into the bar. "Why do you think I need to be protected from you?" I asked. When had I ever needed that?

He dropped his gaze this time, and I thought he was going to shut me out, but instead, he ran the backs of his fingers down my arm and over my hand in a gentle caress. "I've done a lot. Things that damaged me. I thought I was too broken ever to feel this way again. I didn't think my blackened soul could need, want, desire, anyone again."

Although I wanted to know what he had done, that wasn't what I was clinging to at the moment. He wanted, needed, and desired me.

"I think you brought a piece of me back to life. The biggest piece of me. The piece I lost when I thought you were gone. I feel so much more than I've felt in a long time." His hand slipped into mine, and I let him thread our fingers together.

"What are we doing?" I asked.

"Everything. We're doing everything. I'm all in. I've always been all in with you. That hasn't changed."

Wow. Not what I expected. "What does 'all in' mean?" I asked. I didn't want to hope for anything.

He cupped my face with his free hand. His other hand was still holding mine. "I want you. I want our daughter. I want to be more than a part of your lives. I want to be *in* your lives. But right now, I want you. I want you so damn bad I can't focus."

My mouth opened slightly as I stared up at him.

"Come out to my truck. I just need to touch you a little, Addy. Please," he begged, pulling me toward him. He didn't kiss me. He kept his gaze locked on mine as he waited for me to reply.

Franny was a deep sleeper. Going out to his truck was safe. She couldn't hear us out there. "OK," I whispered.

He closed his eyes for a moment, and then his hand tightened around mine as he moved so quickly I almost lost my balance. He all but pulled me behind him out the door. When we got to the steps, he scooped me up and took several long strides until he was at his truck, jerking the door open.

I fell back on my elbows onto the backseat and stared at him as he hovered over me. His eyes slowly roved down my body, until they landed on the hem of my sundress, which rode up as I slid back, exposing my bare thighs and a glimpse of the matching red panties underneath.

"Red," he said, then looked up at me. "They're fucking red. I was tormented all night by what color they might be. Never imagined they'd match this sexy little dress."

The dress wasn't sexy. It was a simple red sundress. I liked the way it fit.

He watched my face as he ran his hand up my leg. His fingers slid just inside my closed thighs, and he pushed them open. "I want this," he said, lowering his mouth to mine.

I wanted this, too, and if he didn't give it to me, I was going to take it.

His mouth touched mine, and I arched up to taste him. I loved his lips. The more he kissed me, the more obsessed I became with them. I wanted to nibble them and lick them. I wanted to feel them on my body. I trembled as my thoughts became naughtier than I'd let them be in a long time.

Captain moved his hand up until his finger brushed the satin crotch of my panties. I was soaked, and I knew it, but it had been so long, and I wanted him so badly I couldn't help it.

He broke the kiss but didn't move from my lips. "So wet. That's fucking hot. I'm gonna need to taste that, baby."

I wanted to plead for him to do just that, but I whimpered instead. Which was all he needed.

Captain swore with a growl, and then both his hands were under my dress, tugging my panties down my legs. I lifted my hips and legs, helping him to free me from the unwanted barrier.

He lifted the panties to his nose and sniffed then with a wicked smile, then folded them carefully and laid them on his dashboard like he had all the time in the world. I wiggled, needing something. The gesture was sweet and really sexy, but my body felt like it was on fire.

"Easy," he said, sliding a hand up my leg. "I'll make it feel good. I swear." Then he lifted my leg and put it over his shoulder before doing the same with my other leg.

I stopped breathing as he held my gaze, lowering his head until that first touch almost sent me flying off the seat. I cried out, but his tongue slid against my swollen clit again, and I began moaning. This was too good. I'd been without for so long, and this was going to be too much. My hands grabbed fistfuls of his long hair as he continued his sweet torment, tasting me.

With each lick, I wanted to claw at something. Beg and plead. The pleasure was building fast, and my body was ready for what was coming. When the heat exploded inside me, I threw back my head, my body trembling, as Captain continued his intimate kissing throughout the experience.

When I came down off my high, he kissed my inner thigh and slowly moved my legs off his shoulders and climbed up to cover me. Through my blissful haze, I stared up at him.

The grin on his face made me giggle. He was inwardly gloating that he'd made me lose control like that. I felt so good I didn't care. He could gloat all he wanted. If I could just have some more of that again.

"Feel good?" he asked, rubbing my bottom lip with his thumb.

I nodded. The goofy smile on my face couldn't be helped.

"You tasted incredible," he said, his voice hoarse. "So good I could go taste some more."

I liked that idea a lot.

The evidence of his arousal was pressed against my thigh. His jeans were still on, but I could feel the rigidness, and I wanted that, too. I wanted to make him feel as good as he'd made me feel.

I moved my thigh so that it rubbed against his erection, and he hissed through his teeth.

"It's my turn," I said, moving again. He moved his hips this time, causing the friction himself.

"No turns. This is all you tonight. I wanted that," he said, pinning me down so I couldn't reach his fly and free what I wanted.

"But I want to," I said, letting my legs fall open so that he was between them. All he had to do was move up just a little to press against where I wanted him to be.

"Fuck, Addy," he said breathlessly, shifting his hips so that my heat was against his.

I wanted more than this. I wanted to give him more. "Let me," I said, moving my hand down to cup him through his jeans. He closed his eyes as I moved my hand over his stiff-

ness. "I want to touch it," I said, trying to get his pants un-
buttoned.

He opened his eyes and looked down at me. The need
made me shiver and grip him harder. His jaw clenched. "What
is it you want?" he asked, moving his hips.

"I want your cock in my mouth," I told him boldly, as I
gently squeezed.

He let out a groan and moved back off me until he was sitting up. I hurried to move to my knees beside him before he
changed his mind. "Didn't mean for you to do this, but fuck
me if I can turn you down when you ask like that."

I quickly got his jeans down until I had him bare in my
hands. He hissed through his teeth again, and his head hit
the back of the seat, but he didn't take his eyes off me. I liked
knowing he wanted to watch me do this. Lowering my mouth,
I kissed the tip, and he trembled under my touch. I loved the
power it gave me.

I wanted to make him tremble. I wanted him to come apart
from my mouth the way I had done for him. The idea excited
me, and I felt the heat between my legs begin to tingle again. I
moved my legs slightly apart and gripped the base of his cock
with one hand, then slid my other hand between my own legs
to tease the sweet ache that was back.

"Fuuuuck," he groaned, and I looked up to see him watching
me touch myself. "I'll fucking come just watching that, baby."

Smiling, I slid my lips down him until the head hit the
back of my throat, making me gag.

"Easy, baby. Don't hurt yourself. I don't want you to do
that." The concern in his voice was laced with a thickness that

told me that as much as he didn't want me hurting myself, he was enjoying it, too.

I sucked hard as I pulled him from my mouth with a pop. "I like it that way," I told him, then took him back into my mouth while his own went slack.

He was completely in my power.

Captain

I like it that way.

What the fuck did that mean? She'd said she hadn't been with anyone else, and the last time she did this, she didn't gag herself. I watched her as the head of my swollen cock slid into her throat. At the moment, I couldn't fucking worry about what she meant.

God, she was gorgeous.

I shifted my attention to the hand she had between her open thighs, and my dick throbbed in her tight, hot mouth. Never had a blow job felt this damn good. She wasn't an expert, but the fact that she was giving it everything she had, while her round ass was up in the air as she got herself off, was making this my own personal fantasy come true.

She moaned, and the vibration made me clench my abs in an attempt to keep from going off in her mouth. I couldn't do that to her. I never did back when we were younger.

Her tongue came out and flicked my sensitive head, and I grabbed a handful of her hair and pulled her off me. "I'm gonna come," I panted, needing to keep from shooting off in her face.

She looked up at me as she shoved my cock down her

throat, just as she got off on her hand, trembling and moaning. I lost it. Holding her head but not wanting her to stop now, I shot my release down her throat, and she took it all, not once coming up or gagging.

"Fuck, Addy, fuck, baby," I growled as the pleasure rocked me. Watching her take all of me had me wanting to turn this dirty. The kind of dirty I liked. The idea only made my cock twitch back to life as she slowly pulled her lips up and let me go with a smile before she licked the little that had leaked out.

The pleased smile on her face was so damn adorable. I reached for the hand that had been between her legs and grabbed her wrist, bringing it to my mouth so I could suck her fingers.

"Oh," she murmured, watching me, her thighs still open as she knelt on the seat, watching me.

When I had her fingers clean, I dropped her hand and asked the one thing I really fucking needed to know but was afraid to ask. "How did you know you liked to gag?" I asked.

She frowned at first, then understanding dawned on her, and she grinned, ducking her head shyly. How could she get shy on me now, after all this? "Just because I haven't been with another man doesn't mean I haven't used my imagination to get some release."

I wasn't sure I liked that answer. "And who were you picturing?" I asked, still needing to hear it had only been me. Even if that was unfair, I couldn't help it.

With the most sincere expression I'd ever seen, she said simply, "You. Who else would I fantasize over?"

I reached for her and pulled her onto my lap and claimed her mouth.

When she pressed her wet, bare pussy over my semihard cock, I had to break the kiss to move her back. If she did that, I'd end up fucking her right here in the backseat, and we'd be in this truck all night. That wasn't where I wanted us to be the first time we slept together again. She deserved more. I'd already let her suck me off. I had to control myself. She wasn't some slut. She was my Addy.

"No. Not here. Not like this." My voice was affected. The needing ache was impossible to miss. Addy scooted closer as I set her back. Pushing her away went against every instinct I had, but I wasn't letting it happen this way. I'd hate myself for it. "Addy, baby, not in this damn truck. At least, not the first time."

"This isn't the first time, or did you forget?" she asked, tilting her head to the side with a teasing grin.

"I never forgot that. Never will," I replied, reaching up to cup the side of her face. "Always this face." I didn't say more. She knew what I meant. Neither of us needed me to explain.

She closed her eyes and leaned into my touch. "OK," she whispered.

Needing this woman had never changed for me. When she was a girl, I'd needed her to complete me. So I could survive. Now that I had her in my arms again, I still needed her. This was how it felt to be whole. It had been so long since I had this feeling that I'd forgotten what it was like.

Addy slid off my lap and sat on the seat beside me. "I need to go back inside in case Franny wakes up," she explained, and reached for the door handle.

"I'll walk you inside," I said, opening the truck door on my side and hopping out, then reaching inside to take her hand.

She slid her hand into mine, and I wanted to keep it there forever. Holding on to this. Part of me feared I'd wake up soon and this would all be a dream. That I wouldn't have Addy or Franny. That my life would still be devoid of emotion. Devoid of need.

"What's that look for?" she asked.

I shook off those thoughts and tightened my hold on her hand as I started walking toward her door. "Nothing."

That wasn't enough for her, though. She stopped walking and tugged on my arm to get my attention. "Don't say nothing. I know that frown. It's the 'River is thinking unhappy thoughts' frown. What are you thinking?"

Once, I had been able to tell her everything. I knew I wouldn't be able to do that now. I had darkness in my life that she'd never understand. I couldn't share those things, not if I wanted to keep her in my life. I had to be worthy of her and Franny. My past was something that would have to stay a secret.

"Just don't want to wake up and find out this is all a dream," I replied finally. Every truth I could tell her, I would. It would make up for the lies I would also have to tell.

Her small hand squeezed mine. "Me, too."

"I've got a lot to make up for. I've changed, but not when it comes to you. Being with you takes me back to the me I thought I'd lost."

I just hoped she believed me and saw that, too. Walking away tonight scared me. Once she had time to think about the asshole I'd been since she arrived, she might regret this.

I wasn't losing her. Not again.

Addy

How did you know you liked to gag?

I covered my face with my hands and groaned in embarrassment. Last night, I'd been so worked up from being in River's arms again I hadn't even thought about what I was doing. In the light of day, I replayed everything in my head. I didn't even know that girl I'd become.

I heard Franny in the kitchen and pushed thoughts of River out of my head. I had to focus on today. Last night meant something to me. I just wasn't sure what it meant to him. Especially after he had time to sleep on it. This afternoon at work would answer my questions. How he acted toward me would tell me if I'd been an idiot or if he had felt what I had felt. The way he had looked at me before he left made me want to believe he was where I was.

"Mommy, you want a waffle?" Franny asked, turning to smile at me as she stood waiting for the toaster to pop out her breakfast.

I shook my head. "No thanks, baby. I think coffee is enough for right now."

"I figured, but I thought I'd ask."

Smiling, I walked over and started a pot.

"When will I see Dad again?"

Good question. We hadn't really discussed that last night. "Soon, I'm sure. He enjoyed being with you as much as you enjoyed being with him," I assured her.

She grinned and sat down at the table. "I think he enjoyed being with you, too. He looks at you a lot."

I set my coffee cup down and composed myself. "Don't get ideas in your head about us, OK?" I needed her to understand. My heart getting broken was one thing, but Franny's heart getting broken was another. I wasn't willing to take that chance.

Last night, I had been with River again, but I couldn't forget that I'd seen the side of him that was Captain. And Captain wasn't someone I was willing to trust all the way. Not yet.

"I'm not getting ideas. I'm just saying I saw him looking at you a lot. Bet if he saw you with your blond hair, he'd really think you were beautiful."

Franny hadn't liked it when I colored my hair red. She'd said I didn't look right. She liked us looking similar.

"I don't think that'll be the case. But I do think it's time I went back to my original color."

Franny started eating, and I drank my coffee, sighing in relief that this conversation was coming to a close.

"When you see him today, will you ask him if he wants to get ice cream with us again?"

She wanted him around so badly. "Why don't I invite him over here for dinner on my next night off? We can cook for him."

Franny beamed at me. "Yes, that's even better. But let's cook him our best stuff. Not just pizza. I can make the biscuits."

"OK. It's a deal," I agreed.

.   .   .

By the time I got to work that afternoon, I was even more unsure. Part of me had expected a call or possibly a text from him. But there had been nothing. Twice, I'd almost texted him to ask him over for dinner, but I'd stopped myself. I wasn't sure what he was thinking, and if he regretted last night, then I wasn't sure I could face him. Especially after what I'd done.

My face flushed with embarrassment yet again, and I ducked my head as I walked through the back entrance.

"You're late." Elle's sharp tone startled me, and I looked up to see her walking out of Captain's office and closing the door behind her.

The sharp pain that shot through me caused me to wince. I didn't want her to think she upset me, but knowing she had been in Captain's office was difficult to take. Especially since I'd heard them in there once having sex.

"I'm five minutes early," I replied. I was never late. She knew that, and she hated it.

"Not by my clock. I'll be writing you up if this happens again."

I wanted to roll my eyes, but I didn't. Taking the high road, I walked past her and toward the lockers in the employee lounge to put my purse away and get my apron. When I walked past Captain's door, I resisted the urge to kick it. I didn't know what she was doing in there, but I hated that I was completely jealous.

Last night had been a mistake. He hadn't texted or called all day, and then I saw his ex leave his office the moment I arrived. If I didn't acknowledge the clues that were being thrown at me, I was being naive. He was Franny's dad. That was it. I wouldn't play this game.

Brad was in the employee lounge, and he turned and smiled at me. "Hey."

"Hey," I replied, surprised that he'd actually spoken to me.

"Last night was crazy busy. Be glad you were off."

Small talk. Something else I hadn't expected. "Yeah? I hope tonight isn't too bad."

"Hope this new guy can handle things when Captain's gone."

Something else I hadn't thought through. Would I keep working here when Captain was gone? Why keep this job and deal with Elle, when I could work somewhere where I didn't have to deal with a mean bitch who hated me?

"I'm sure Captain will have him ready when he leaves," I said to fill the silence. Because right now, I didn't want to think about Captain.

"You're right. I will." Captain's voice came from the doorway. I tensed but didn't turn around to look at him.

"Oh, yeah. I know you will. I just meant that he's not like you. I don't doubt your skills." Brad sounded a little nervous.

"Rose, I need to see you in my office." His voice had softened from the one he'd used with Brad.

"I'm late. If I don't get out to the dining room, your girlfriend will write me up. She told me so when she came out of your office earlier." The bitterness in my tone was obvious. I hadn't meant to say all that, but it just came spilling out. Now I looked like a jealous bitch. Crap.

"Now, Rose." His voice lowered, and I could hear a small warning in his tone.

As much as I wanted to scream at him to go away—because I really did want to throw a total female fit—I nodded and closed my locker with more force than necessary, before turning to follow him to his office.

Except he didn't turn around, and he wasn't walking away. He was watching me, with a frown wrinkling his forehead. He was confused, as he should be. I was completely overreacting. So we had made out last night. It wasn't like we made any promises.

This wasn't high school, but I was acting like a crazy teenage girl.

I sighed. There was nothing I could say about it except that I was sorry. I didn't think my pride was going to let me apologize, though.

Captain turned and headed toward his office. All I could do was fall in step behind him. I could feel Brad's eyes on my retreating back, but there was no way I was saying goodbye to him or even looking at him. I might not be able to make eye contact with him again after this. Somehow I'd managed to embarrass myself even more.

At the first step I took into Captain's office, he turned and wrapped his hand around my wrist and tugged me closer before slamming the door behind me. I jumped, and my pulse quickened under his firm touch. I'd made him angry, but I wasn't scared of him.

"Girlfriend?" he said in a low, gravelly voice, as he backed me up against the door. "Last time I checked, it was *your* pussy I was tasting."

Oh, dear God.

"Elle has no power to do shit to you. Her threats are pointless. I won't let her hurt you, and you know that. You *should* know that." He stopped and lowered his head until his lips kissed my neck. "You getting jealous pisses me off and turns me the fuck on, all at the same time."

Oh, dear God.

His tongue came out, and he ran it along the curve of my neck. "Don't want anyone else. Told you last night it was always your face. Every damn time. I never could love anyone but you."

My body melted against him.

"I tried all there was to try. I did everything I could to get you out of my head. But not one day went by that I didn't miss you. That I didn't see your face when I closed my eyes."

His mouth trailed kisses up my neck, until he placed one small one at the corner of my mouth. Then he rested his forehead against mine and picked me up by the waist until I was at his eye level.

"Tell me what set you off. Was it Elle walking out of my office? Just because she comes in here to bitch doesn't mean I want her here. You need to trust me."

"You didn't call or even text me all day," I blurted out.

A slow smile tugged at his lips, and he shook his head. "I was giving you some space to accept this. Us. Last night was intense, and I didn't want to overwhelm you. But if I'd thought for a second you were waiting for me to call, I'd have fucking called you."

All the worry and jealousy that had been eating me up vanished, and I wrapped my arms around his neck. "I'm sorry."

He chuckled and leaned in to claim my mouth in a kiss that was as sweet as it was hot. I grabbed handfuls of his hair, and his hands gripped me tighter as he pulled me against him. "Wrap your legs around me," he said against my lips.

When I did, he walked me over to the sofa and sank down onto it while holding me. "I think I'll keep you in here all night," he said with a cocky grin.

"I'll definitely get written up then," I replied.

He shrugged. "I know the boss."

Laughing, I leaned in to kiss him again. Because when we were like this, I was home.

Captain

I stood watching Addy in the dining room with one of her tables. I kept trying to focus on work, but I always ended up right back here. She laughed at the older man who was telling her some story that his wife looked amused by as well. She had a charm about her that put everyone at ease. I found myself wanting that all to myself.

"So that's what has you so distracted lately," Blaire's voice whispered beside me. Turning, I looked down at my sister, who was checking out Addy with a grin on her face.

"What are you doing here?" I asked, a little annoyed to be caught by Blaire of all people.

"Coming to find out why you've ignored my last two phone calls and only given me one-word answers to my texts." She nodded her head in Addy's direction. "I like what I see. This is a good reason to ignore me. Bethy said she saw you with an attractive redhead and an adorable little blond girl last night. I thought I'd come see you and ask about it. But I can see for myself instead. So she has a daughter?"

I stepped back into the hallway before Addy could turn and see us looking at her and talking. I hadn't noticed Blaire's friend Bethy in Grayton last night, but then I'd had my eyes on my girls. No one else had mattered.

"Come to my office," I told her. If Blaire was going to ask questions, I wanted some privacy.

"I didn't peg you as someone who'd date a single mom, but I'm liking this side of you."

"The girl, Franny. She's mine." There, I'd said it. I needed to tell someone. I wanted to tell someone. Blaire's eyes went wide, and her mouth fell open as she stared at me.

"Yours?" she asked, still in shock.

"Rose . . . is from my past. A piece of my past that I keep close. It's a long story. I didn't know about Franny until a week ago."

Blaire's eyes flared bright, and she placed her hands on her hips like she was ready to attack someone. "She kept your child from you?"

I shook my head and held up my hand to calm my firecracker sister down. "It's not like that. She couldn't find me. I left that life and ran. Changed my name, made some choices that were bad. Finding me wasn't easy. But she kept looking until she did."

Blaire's stance relaxed, and her expression softened. "Oh, well, that's different."

I nodded. "Yeah. She hasn't had an easy time. I blame myself for that, but she has me now, and I'm not going anywhere."

We stood in silence. I could see the wheels turning in Blaire's head. I just had to wait for her to think it through.

"I want to meet them," she said simply.

"Good. I want them to meet you, too."

Blaire smiled. "I can't believe this."

If she only knew the real story . . . but I'd never tell her. My past was something that would stay between Addy and me. Blaire had just come into my life a few years ago. We shared the same father, but I'd been born to a teenage mother, who gave me up for adoption. When I had decided to find my birth parents, I also found Blaire. A sister I hadn't known I'd had. We were growing closer now, but this was still more than I wanted to share with her.

"And her name isn't actually Rose. It's Addy. She was checking me out to make sure I had turned into a man worthy of our child, so she disguised herself and changed her name."

Blaire's grin grew. "I like her. She's a protective momma. Says a lot about a person."

"Just wait until you meet Franny and see what an amazing job she's done raising her."

"Dinner at my house on your next night off. Make sure you bring both of them." Blaire didn't ask; she just commanded.

"Let me talk to her about it first. Make sure she's good with that. This is all new for us, and I don't want to do anything that's too much for Franny."

Blaire let out a laugh and beamed at me. "You're a daddy. I love this."

I did, too. "Yeah," I replied.

Once I had my sister out of my office, I went back to check on things. It wasn't like I was needed, exactly, but I wanted to see Addy.

"Rose was late getting in today and late to the meeting in the dining room. I'm making the call to let her go," Elle said, walking out of the kitchen and directly toward me.

"No," I replied, annoyed that Elle was attacking Addy out of simple jealousy.

"Why? Are you seeing her? Is that it? If anyone else was this late, you'd let them go. Why does she get away with it?"

I walked around Elle and headed to the dining room.

"Answer me. Is she the one you moved on to?"

I stopped in my tracks, hating the disbelief in her voice, as if she found herself superior to Addy. Stupid girl. I glanced back over my shoulder and met her angry gaze. "She's the best damn server we have here. You know it, and so does everyone else."

As much as I wanted to tell her that yes, I was with Addy, I couldn't do it. She would attack Addy with a ferocity that would end with me firing her and causing shit with Stout.

"She's mediocre at best," Elle snapped.

"Don't be pathetic," I replied, bored with this entire conversation.

"I hate you!" she called out heatedly.

I felt nothing in return, so I had no response.

Addy

He had watched me all night. It had made me feel excited and nervous at the same time. I liked knowing he was there, but I was also worried about forgetting what I was doing if I looked back at him.

I expected him to meet me the moment we closed, but he wasn't there. I went to the back to get my purse, still thinking he'd show up, but he didn't. Elle kept looking my way and smirking, as if there was something she knew that I didn't. I ignored her and decided I would stop by his office to say good night. Maybe he was busy.

His office door was open, and I could see it was empty. I thought about texting him but changed my mind. I needed to get home to Franny. I would wait until he contacted me. Maybe he had been trying to tell me something, but I'd never looked his way to find out what it could be.

There were several scenarios running through my mind, but as I stepped outside, I realized it was none of them; his truck was still there in the parking lot, and so was he. In the darkness, I could see him deep in conversation with a tall blonde, her hair pulled back tightly in a ponytail, dressed in tight black leather. They couldn't be any closer to each other without actually touching. I paused and took them in. Even in the shadows, I could see that Captain's face was intent as he listened to her.

I'd never seen her before, but he seemed to know her. She was important to him. The way his body leaned into hers as he spoke meant something. There was an air of intimacy about them that made my stomach turn.

Captain looked passionate as he spoke, and he leaned in closer toward her. I couldn't stay and watch this any longer. I didn't know what it was, but I could tell just from this little glimpse that it was more than I could accept.

Hurrying to my car, I pulled out my keys and unlocked it. Getting home and holding Franny close would ease this ache. Knowing that she was always there helped me face everything. She came first. She was all that mattered in this world. I didn't need him. She did. But I didn't.

I could survive this. I was stronger than this.

It wasn't until I pulled out onto the road that the tears stung my eyes, and I had to blink them back. Crying over this wasn't something I would accept. Tomorrow, I was sure he'd have some excuse. I didn't think I cared to hear it. Nothing could explain what I had seen.

I held my tears the entire trip home, and when I finally got there, I was so exhausted from the sheer force of will that I all but ran into the house.

Holding Franny all night was what I needed.

He texted three times and called five times within the hour. I ignored them all. Curled up with Franny in bed, I put my phone on silent and watched as it lit up each time. I wasn't answering. If he was so worried about me getting home safely, he should have been there for me when I got off work. Not with the strange blonde. That spoke volumes. He hadn't even noticed me leave. Every time I reminded myself of this, it gave me more strength to stand firm.

"Mommy, why is Dad outside, asleep in his truck?" Franny asked.

I opened my eyes and looked up to find her leaning over me. Trying to comprehend exactly what she had just said, however, took me a moment.

"He's outside sleeping. In his truck," she said, with a confused and anxious expression. "Do I go wake him up?"

Who was outside? "Huh?" I asked, as I sat up and rubbed my eyes, trying to focus on my daughter.

"Dad. In his truck." She was starting to sound frustrated.

"Captain?" I repeated, feeling even more confused than she looked.

Franny let out a sigh. "I'm going to wake him up." Then she turned and ran out of the room.

Captain was outside in his truck. Crap! I jumped up, grabbed a discarded pair of shorts, and tugged them on, along with the tank top I had slept in, before running after Franny. Why Captain would be asleep outside in his truck made no sense to me. I didn't want Franny to be the one to wake him and confront him.

"Franny, wait!" I called out as I chased after her.

She had her hand on the door, about to go outside, when

she stopped and looked back at me. "He's asleep in his truck." She sounded worried.

I nodded that I understood what she was telling me. "Let me see why he's out there. You stay in here and make yourself some breakfast. I'm sure he'll come in when he's awake. Make him a waffle, too," I suggested, hoping this would keep her in the house.

She looked torn as she glanced back at the window. "OK, but make sure he comes inside. I want to see him. He's here to see me, I think."

"I will. I promise," I assured her.

I didn't give her time to argue before I headed outside toward Captain's truck. I knew Franny would be watching from the window, so yelling at him wasn't an option.

The fact that he was here infuriated me. He was manipulating me. He knew I wouldn't react badly in front of Franny. Besides, what was the point in sleeping out here all night? I hadn't answered his calls; that should have been enough for him to get the point.

Watching him asleep, with his head tilted back against the seat, didn't help my temper. He even looked good sleeping. That wasn't fair. Damn him.

I knocked hard on the window and silently enjoyed watching him jerk awake at the sudden sound. I didn't give him time to wake up before I knocked again and glared at him. Franny was watching, but I was far enough away that she couldn't see my face.

Captain sat up and went to open his door. I stepped back, crossing my arms over my chest defensively.

"What are you doing?" I demanded, before he could say anything.

"You didn't answer your phone."

"So it makes sense for you to sleep in your truck in my driveway? Franny's inside right now, worried about you and making you waffles. Which means you're going in there and eating the damn waffles with her. Assure her you're fine, and come up with some reason for why you felt compelled to sleep in my driveway."

Captain glanced back at the house, and I saw a glimpse of regret on his face for worrying Franny. At least there was that. Now he had some clue to how dumb this was.

"Why didn't you answer?" he asked, looking back at me. His hair was mussed from sleeping, and I wanted to reach up and fix it. But I wouldn't. I wasn't touching this man again.

"I was in bed. If you'd wanted to talk to me, you should have done that before I left work. I wasn't available to chat once I got home. That time is reserved for Franny." I glared at him, waiting for him to give me a credible reason. Some stupid excuse. There was nothing he could say that would make me not feel hurt by what I'd seen.

"You're angry," he said, taking a step closer to me.

I just laughed. How could I respond to that? "Come inside and eat waffles with our daughter. Then leave." I turned to walk back to the house.

"Why are you mad? Did you see me talking to Alexa last night? Is that what this is about?"

Great, she had a name. "If that's the blonde's name, then yeah," I replied, not slowing down.

"She's an old friend."

"Good for you."

"Addy, stop. Seriously, listen to me."

I didn't stop. I was too mad at Alexa for being an old friend and at myself for caring.

"Addy," he called out again. "Don't do this."

"I'm going to eat with Franny. She's watching us right now."

He didn't say anything more, but I could hear his footsteps behind me. I looked up to see Franny peeking out the window, like I knew she would be.

"Tell me you'll let me explain what you think you saw before we go in there," he said, in a low voice that Franny wouldn't be able to hear from inside.

"Nothing to explain," I replied, still not ready to soften up. The fact that he had slept outside my house wasn't enough to fix this. If I had to deal with women at his car, in his office, and God knew where else, then I wasn't doing this. I would not compete for his attention.

"Just make Franny happy, Captain. That's all I require from you," I said with a smile, for my daughter's sake, then headed into the house.

Franny was running back to the toaster when the door opened. "I'm making waffles," she announced, for Captain's benefit, not mine.

"I'll have two," I told her. She glanced back at me and smiled, surprised that I was eating, but didn't question it.

"I'll have three," Captain said, walking in behind me.

"OK!" Franny said, and she lit up as if her favorite celebrity had just walked into the house.

I wouldn't let him hurt her, too. I had allowed him into her world, and he would be what she needed. I would make sure of that.

Captain

She was pissed, and I had no idea how the fuck I was going to explain this. Alexa worked for DeCarlo. She'd been with him almost as long as I had, but she had no plans to get out. There were few people in this world who were as ruthless as Alexa. She was a trained killer, and no one saw her coming, because she played the part well.

Her easiest targets were men, simply because she could use her body and her looks to reel them in before she offed them. It was easier for her to hit her marks, but she did it with no emotion. I'd watched her do it more than once, and it was intense, the way she killed without even an ounce of remorse.

Last night, she had come to the restaurant to let me know that members of a gang were believed to be coming after me. They had some insider info on who had killed their "brother," and they wanted payback.

Knowing there was a possibility that my past was coming back to ruin things now was the scariest shit I'd ever had to swallow. If they had been watching me, it wouldn't take much for them to figure out who Addy and Franny were. I had come here last night to make sure they were safe. When Addy hadn't answered, I hadn't left. I wasn't leaving them alone until Cope and Alexa found the bastards who were looking for me.

Both of them were in town, trailing who they believed was here for me. If Cope had come to see me and let me in on all this shit, then I wouldn't have Addy upset with me. But he'd sent Alexa while he kept tracking.

Fucking hell. The only excuse I had for Addy was that Alexa was an old friend. Telling her the truth wasn't something I was willing to do. I'd lose her if she knew. She would take our daughter and run like hell.

And who could blame her?

I looked across the table at my daughter, as she chatted happily, completely oblivious that her mother was ready to stab me with the fork she was innocently eating her waffles with.

"It's time for you to get dressed for school," Addy said when Franny got to a stopping point.

"OK, but can Dad take me?" she asked, looking from her mother to me hopefully.

"I'd love to take you," I said, before Addy could respond. Hearing Franny call me Dad so easily made my chest swell.

Addy nodded. "That's fine with me. Now, hurry so he doesn't have to rush to get you there on time."

"I will!" she said, jumping up from her chair and hurrying back to the bedroom.

I turned my attention to Addy, who was clearing the table before Franny had even completely left the room.

"You're not even going to look at me?" I asked, needing her eyes on me so she could see how fucking sincere I was about this situation.

"No reason to," was her response.

"Addy, please," I begged.

She paused from picking up Franny's plate and finally lifted her eyes to meet mine. "What?"

I had her attention now, and not fucking it up was more pressure than I expected. It was like I had five seconds to keep her attention, and the heat was on. "When I tell you she's an old friend, I mean it. She's in town with another friend of mine. A guy. They're together. They had some info for me regarding my old job. That's it."

I was more than positive that Cope and Alexa had fucked around. So it wasn't a complete lie. I was insinuating that they were more, but it was the best thing I could come up with, and from the look in Addy's eyes, she seemed to be buying it, so I kept going.

"I thought I'd see you leave. When I realized your car was gone, I started calling, but then you wouldn't answer. I was worried, and I wanted to see you, so I came here. Sleeping outside was the only way I could find any peace. I needed to hear your voice."

"Can I wear this?" Franny asked.

Addy blinked and moved away from the table to turn and look at our daughter. "Yes, that's good. Why don't you wear your white tennis shoes with it?"

Franny nodded and hurried back to the room.

"Can I come back here after I take her to school?"

She didn't look at me but instead stared straight ahead. "I don't know, Captain."

"Addy, you've got to believe me."

She turned to look at me, and there was obvious fear in her

eyes. She was scared to trust me. "She needs you. I want you in our life. But I'm scared to need you, too."

I had stood up and started to move toward her when Franny came skipping into the room with her book bag on her shoulder. "Ready!"

Addy went back to cleaning up. "Don't forget your lunchbox in the fridge."

Franny ran over to the fridge and got out a pink polka-dot lunchbox, then went over to Addy and wrapped her arms around her waist.

Addy turned and bent down to pull her in for a hug. "Have a wonderful day. Make it matter," she said.

Franny nodded. "I got this," she assured her mother. They released each other, and Franny walked over to me. "Let's go."

Addy's gaze met mine, and she gave me a simple nod. That was all the encouragement I needed.

Addy

I had done it again. I had jumped to conclusions. I didn't let him explain. When had I stopped trusting? When had I gotten so negative? I asked myself these questions and more while I cleaned the kitchen and took a shower before Captain returned.

The fact that he had slept outside simply because I wouldn't answer his calls was proof enough that he cared and I was being an asshole. After all this time, I was still so incredibly jealous and insecure with him. I didn't want to be that way. He never gave me a reason not to trust him, back then or now. I had to stop it.

By the time I was out of the shower and dressed, Captain was knocking on my door. I had some apologizing to do, and this would be the last time I did this. Next time, I was asking him if I saw something, not sulking and getting upset.

When I opened the door, Captain walked in, his gaze intent on me. "You gotta stop doing this to me, Addy. After everything that's happened over the past two days and everything I've said to you, I would think you'd know where my head and my heart are. Where they have always been."

"I know," I agreed.

He opened his mouth to say something and stopped when my response sank in.

"I won't do it again," I assured him.

He took a step closer. "I don't like thinking you're upset with me."

I took a step back, not sure what he was doing. But he took another step, closing the distance. "Can't love anyone but you." His frown faded into something deeper. Something intense.

My heart squeezed at his words, and it was hard to think of anything else. When his hands wrapped around my waist and tugged me close, I went willingly. This was my River. The boy who stole my heart and never gave it back.

"Come here," he said softly, before his mouth pressed against mine.

I slipped my hands up his chest and held on to his shoulders while standing on my tiptoes. It was as high as I could reach.

"So tiny," he murmured against my lips, then picked me up and walked us over to the bar. He set me on it so that my mouth was level with his. "I always wanted to hold you close and protect you. I couldn't. But God, I wanted to. I failed you so many times. For ten years, I was empty . . . broken." He stopped and closed his eyes, then took a deep breath. "I thought I'd lost you. I lived without you, fighting demons I couldn't kill."

I moved my hand to touch the side of his stubbled jaw gently. "I'm here now. No more demons to fight."

I watched his throat as he swallowed hard and gave me a small nod, but there was something in his eyes that worried me. Before I could look closer and figure out what was wrong, his hands tightened their hold on my hips, and he tugged me closer to him. "I need you," he said in a soft growl.

I needed him, too. I had needed him for ten years. In many ways. But right now, I knew that the way he meant was the way I needed him the most. I would always need him this way. Just him.

Lifting my legs, I wrapped them around his waist.

"Let me take you to the bed," he whispered, as he kissed my ear.

"No." I shook my head. "Do it here."

He stilled, and I ran my hands underneath his shirt to feel his muscled chest.

"On the counter?" he asked, pulling back just enough to lock eyes with me.

I nodded, biting my lip because I'd never done something like this before. I wanted to. I wanted to know what wild, uninhibited sex felt like. I was a grown woman and a mother, but I'd never experienced such things. Things I only wanted to experience with River.

His hands clasped my thighs and jerked me close enough that I could feel his erection pressed between my legs. My clit pulsed with excitement. This was real. Not my fantasy. It was better.

With a low growl, his mouth covered mine again, and I held on to his sides, feeling his muscles flex under my touch. The smell of his skin was intoxicating, and I felt light-headed from inhaling so quickly, trying to get more of him. I loved having him cover my body with his. I loved feeling like we were connected.

It wasn't until he whispered "Lift your arms" that I realized he was taking my shirt off. I obeyed, quivering with excitement. When his hands covered my breasts and squeezed their fullness, I couldn't keep from moaning. It felt so good. The ache in my nipples shot straight to my core, and I could feel the dampness in my panties. It was like he was slowly lighting a firecracker; at any moment, he would touch the right spot, and I'd fall apart.

He unhooked my bra with one hand and slowly pulled it away, dropping it to the floor. "So fucking beautiful," he murmured, his eyes taking in my naked breasts. My nipples were so hard I was afraid if he touched one, I'd come. Not that I didn't want to have an orgasm, but how pathetic would I look if I did?

His hands moved to hold them, and he brushed his thumb over the sensitive crests. I never wanted this to be over. Being touched by him this way was enough. More than I could have hoped for.

He kissed his way down my neck, and I leaned back, arching my neck so he could have more access. I wanted his mouth everywhere. Taking me to places I'd never been and places I just wanted to be with him.

Captain

Finding the strength to take this slowly was the hardest thing I'd ever done. I didn't want to take this slowly. I wanted Addy naked and wrapped around me while I buried myself so deep in her that I got lost. My body trembled when I thought about how that was going to feel.

Life without her had been hell, but having her now, I realized I'd found my heaven. I'd made it through. Losing her now was impossible. I'd never make it. She wasn't the kind you could survive losing twice.

Sliding my hand up her inner thigh until I could feel the dampness of her panties, I held my breath.

"Please, now," she said, her nails biting into my arms. "I want you inside me."

Inhaling deeply, I could smell her arousal, and my cock throbbed. "Off," I growled, as I lifted her ass to tug her panties down her legs and toss them onto the floor.

Her hands were shaking as she worked on the button of my jeans. As much as I wanted to watch her undress me, all I could think about was how hot she'd felt when I'd slid my fingers over her.

I helped her unfasten my jeans and push them down my hips.

"I'm on the pill," she said, touching my lower stomach with reverence. "Can we . . . do it without a condom?"

I knew I was clean. I kept myself checked, and I had been sure to check myself out after the relationship with Elle ended.

I held her legs open wider and went from watching us slowly come together to looking into her fascinated face, as I slowly moved to enter her. I had touched her. I knew how tight she was. It was all that was keeping me from slamming into her with the need clawing at my body.

Her loud gasp was followed by her hands tightening around my arms and her eyes flaring hot with excitement. Sliding into her was another level of pure bliss. A low groan broke from my chest, as her tightness squeezed me with each inch that I sank deeper. Addy's legs gripped me tightly around the waist, and the panting noises she was making only made it hotter.

"You're so fucking tight," I said through clenched teeth.

"I'm sorry," she whispered, looking up at me with concern in her eyes.

I lowered my mouth to touch hers. "Don't apologize for being goddamn perfect, Addy. You feel so good I'm close to going crazy."

She let go of my arms and slid them around my neck, and her mouth made a small "oh" the second I was completely buried in her. "Oh, God," she said, clinging to me while pressing her bare chest against mine.

"That's it." I closed my eyes and let the completeness of the moment sink in.

When I rocked my hips back, she made sexy little sounds

that made my balls clench tighter. I was going to explode way too soon if she didn't stop with the sexy shit.

"Feel good?" I asked her, needing it to feel good to her more than anything else.

"Yes, oh, yes, so good," she said into my neck, where her face was now tucked. Her tongue came out and took a small lick against my skin.

Our bodies began to move in perfect rhythm. Her skin pressed against mine, and her tightness squeezed my cock with each throb and pulse. I knew the moment she came, I would be finished. I'd never be able to hold out on finishing with her.

Her hand slid down my chest and rested on my abs. She looked down to watch us just before her body stiffened and began to tremble. Lifting her head, she looked up at me. Her mouth was slightly open, and her eyes were closing. The hand on my abs fisted as she cried out my name. Not Captain but River.

And with that, I followed her over the edge.

Two hours later, I held Addy in her bed while she slept. After I'd recovered in the kitchen, I had carried her in here, and we'd made love again. This time, slower and more thoroughly. I had managed to let her get off twice before I went with her. She had then closed her eyes and curled into me before drifting off into an exhausted sleep.

Something else I had missed. Holding Addy while she slept had been a part of my life. It was what helped me sleep at night. Without her in my arms, sleeping had almost been impossible for years.

I stared at the ceiling. My past was back to haunt me, and it wasn't leaving. I had to face it and find a way to keep Addy, too. She and Franny were my life. I had promised myself that I was done with killing. But if someone threatened what I loved most, I'd remind them who they were dealing with. I'd do anything to protect my girls.

My phone vibrated on the table beside me. I reached over for it gently so as not to disturb Addy.

It was DeCarlo. "They're there. You'll have to take them out."

That was it. Nothing more. But I knew exactly what he was talking about. My last job wasn't over yet.

Major

It was dark as shit. I hated working in the dark. Times like this, I wondered what the hell I'd gotten myself into. I had craved danger and excitement. Something more than what I had. But was *this* really what I wanted?

Working with Captain had been cool. He wasn't a cold-blooded killer. The man had compassion and knew when to draw a line and stand on one side of it.

Cope, however, was a fucking maniac. I swear, the dude killed for fun. He never acted like it affected him or like he regretted one moment. And this was the man I was supposed to get my marching orders from.

Fuck my life.

"Captain's been alerted. This will end soon." Cope's voice came from the shadows. Dammit. He always came out of no-where. Never could hear the son of a bitch. He was like a damn ninja.

"How's it gonna go over? We locate them?" I asked, annoyed that he'd once again snuck up on me when I was actively attempting to be alert.

"Alexa has them on target. Captain will go to her and take them out."

Captain had said he was done with killing. The fact that he had to come in because of an old job didn't sit well with me. I wanted to know that when I walked away, I would be truly free.

"He ain't working anymore," I replied. "Why can't we do it? Hell, I'll do it."

Cope lit a cigarette and shrugged as he stared out at the old house I'd been instructed to watch. "You're right. But this is his problem. We tracked them and made sure he knew, because Benedetto takes care of his own. Captain might be out, but he's still got blood on his hands for DeCarlo. We have his back, but he knows the kill is his responsibility."

Seemed screwed-up to me. I still didn't understand all the inner workings of this thing. What I did know was that De-Carlo wasn't completely on the up and up. There was some-thing else going on, other than offing men who deserved it. All I got was orders from Cope, and so far, I hadn't been able to close a deal on my own.

"The girl you're watching is who you need to focus on. We think she knows what we need. I'll give you the details tomor-row. Tonight we end this for Cap."

The job I was sent here for was getting more and more complicated. I wasn't even sure what the details were yet. Just that there was a man we were searching for who had abducted a kid ten years ago and gotten away with it. I'd been told noth-ing more.

Cope reached for his phone and checked the screen. "He's there. Alexa has armed him, and he's going in. Let's move that way in case he needs more backup," Cope said, dropping the lit cigarette and stomping on it. He began moving toward the forest behind us.

"What about the house?" I asked, when I turned to follow him.

"Ain't no one there of importance. Just needed you in a prime location, and I figured this would keep you busy," he replied in a bored tone.

Fucker. He really was annoying as hell. I'd been out here watching this house for three hours and had about a million mosquito bites to show for it.

"When you planning on giving me more credit?" I asked, annoyed. Everyone was so scared of Cope, but he only killed those he was told to kill. He followed orders, same as everyone else.

"When you do the fucking job you're given," he replied, as he continued to move forward. "Now, shut the fuck up, and stop bitching like a woman. Focus. Cap might need us."

I wanted to argue or at least call him a motherfucker, but I kept my mouth shut. I hadn't actually been given a job that was easy. Being told to stalk my cousin's sister was messed-up. Didn't help that I'd already had my eyes on her before I signed on for all this shit. Nan was a hot piece of ass. But if she was fucking around with someone DeCarlo wanted, then she was in danger.

And I couldn't even tell Mase about it if I wanted either of us to live.

Addy

After the most amazing morning of my life, I had woken up to Captain being distant and awkward. I hadn't been expecting him to withdraw like that. When we were younger, we had become more attached every time we slept together. This experience was completely different.

His thoughts had been elsewhere. When he had given me an excuse that he had to get to work to deal with some things, his eyes said something else. I felt like I'd been given the brush-off. My stomach was twisted in a knot for the rest of the day.

Franny coming home had helped brighten things some. Having her talk about her day and hearing her laugh at her favorite television shows was a definite distraction. I didn't have to work that night, and for that I was thankful. Facing Captain now seemed impossible.

I wasn't sure what to say to him or even how to look at him. He had kissed me goodbye and said he'd call me soon. That was it. Then he'd just gotten out of here as fast as possible.

Franny's constant talk about how much fun she'd had when he took her to school that morning didn't help. When she finally stopped talking about him and started on her homework, I was relieved.

I focused on making dinner, even though I didn't have an appetite. I hadn't had one all day. There was no room in my stomach for anything but that knot he'd left there.

When Franny's bedtime finally rolled around and I hadn't even gotten a text from Captain, I was devastated. Smiling and tucking her in like my heart wasn't slowly breaking open was hard, but I'd managed it.

It wasn't until I knew she'd fallen asleep that I curled up on the sofa with my phone in my hand and let the first tear slowly fall. I knew he was busy, and I knew what his work was like, but I also knew that if he'd wanted to, he would have found a moment to at least text me something, anything. Anything at all would have been nice.

A knock at the door startled me, and I jumped up and wiped my eyes. Maybe it was Captain, and he'd come to see me and explain why he hadn't called all day. I hurried over to the door and opened it, expecting Captain, but froze when an extremely tall and terrifying man, with the widest shoulders I'd ever seen, locked his cold, steel-blue eyes on me.

I gripped my phone tightly in my hand. I had no idea who this man was, but I had a feeling that I'd need the phone to dial 911. I wondered if I could do it fast enough.

"Stop hatching an escape plan. I'm not here to hurt you. Get your neighbor over there to watch your kid, and come with me. Captain needs you."

What? I stared up at the man, wondering how he could be that attractive and scary as hell all at once. And how he knew about my neighbor and my kid.

"We need to go. Get your girl taken care of, and let's move," he said with authority.

"Excuse me, but who are you?" I asked, taking a step back, with my hand on the doorknob.

He sighed as if I was exhausting him. "Knew I should have sent Alexa," he grumbled. Then, with an irritated glance, he pointed to the bedroom where Franny was sleeping. "Your daughter needs your neighbor to stay with her. I need to take you to the fucking hospital, because Captain had some bad shit go down tonight. When he wakes his ass up, he's gonna want to see his woman. Now, would you please do as I tell you, and stop asking me a million damn questions?"

Two things I never wanted to hear in my life were "Captain" and "hospital" together in one sentence. Maybe it was stupidity, or maybe it was fear for Captain . . . or maybe I just couldn't imagine that someone who wanted to harm me would talk to me like a disobedient child, but I pulled out my phone, keeping my eyes on the large man the whole time, and dialed Mrs. Baylor's number.

"Better be your neighbor you're calling," he muttered.

Diana answered on the second ring. "Rose, you OK?"

"Yes, Mrs. Baylor, I'm fine. But I need to visit a friend who has been put in the hospital. Could you please come stay here with Franny? She's already sleeping."

I could see the relief on the man's face as he nodded and walked back into the darkness to a black truck that I almost couldn't see, even in the moonlight.

"Oh, my goodness. I hope everything is OK. I'll be right there."

"Thank you," I replied before hanging up. I walked out onto the porch. "How do you know Captain?" I asked the man.

"Worked together."

I couldn't picture this man working in a restaurant of any kind, but then, Captain didn't really fit into the industry himself, either. "At the restaurant here?" I asked, knowing that if he said yes, he was lying.

What sounded like a muffled chuckle came first. "Fuck no" was the only response I got before he climbed back into his truck.

Mrs. Baylor hurried across the yard and patted my back when she got up the porch steps. "I got her. You go see about your friend."

I thanked her again with a hug and hurried down the steps to the truck—and a stranger I was choosing to trust completely.

Once I was in the truck, I buckled and turned to study the man already pulling out onto the road.

"Just because she looks harmless, that doesn't mean she's not a smart woman. Don't think she didn't take in the make and model of this truck and look at your license plate before we drove off. If I don't come back, she'll report you to the police."

A very small, almost elusive smirk touched the corner of his mouth. "Good" was his only reply, before his face went back to complete neutrality. As odd as he was, that response was comforting.

"Could you tell me your name, please?" I asked.

He scowled. "Cope."

Cope? Was that a name? "Cope like Copeland?" I asked.

"Cope like Cope" was his reply.

Well, OK, then. "Nice to meet you, Cope. I'm—"

"Addison Turner. You lived in River Kipling's home as a foster child for four years. His mother was batshit crazy and abused you. I know everything about you, so save it."

My mouth dropped open as I listened to this man sum up my whole past with River in four sentences. How did he know this? Was he really that close to River? "So Captain is really in the hospital? This is true?"

He nodded and kept scowling.

"He's going to be OK, though?" I asked, my heart starting to beat faster and my fear clawing its way to the top. Although I had gotten into this truck, I wasn't so sure he was being honest with me.

"Fuck yeah. Cap's survived more than a flyaway bullet to the leg. He'll be fine, but he's gonna want you."

Flyaway . . . *"What?"* I asked, grabbing the handle of the door as the word "bullet" sank in. Someone had shot him? How? Why? He was at work tonight.

"Reckon ain't my shit to share with you. Cap will have to do that. But yeah, he's gonna be fine. He'll even get to keep his leg. Clean shot through."

Keep his leg . . . clean shot through. Oh, dear God.

I didn't say much more as I watched him drive in the direction of the hospital. A very large part of me was thinking I'd rather he had come to abduct me than escort me to the hospital where Captain was lying, shot up half to death.

When he pulled into the parking lot, I almost jumped out of the moving truck.

"Whoa, woman. Seriously, chill the fuck out. I'll get you up there quick," he barked at me when I started to open the door.

"I need to get to him," I snapped back.

"And I'll get you there. Jesus," he grumbled, as he opened his truck door and I jumped down from my seat.

This guy had better hurry, or I was leaving him here and heading straight for the information desk. I didn't have time for him to take his time.

"Room 345. Go on. I need coffee," he said, as if he could read my mind.

I didn't even turn back and look at him before I broke into a run.

Captain

Keeping my eyes open was fucking hard. The pain meds they had me on were intense. I'd felt the bullet tear through my leg when the jackass went down with one last pull of his trigger. My mind hadn't been on the fact that my leg was shot though. All I'd cared about was that I was going to live. I wasn't leaving Addy and Franny.

It wasn't the first time I'd been shot, but it was the first time I didn't want to die. I had something to live for now. That changed everything. I had killed two men tonight. Cope had taken out the third when I'd gone down with my leg.

This was my end to it. I had a family now, and this life was not what I wanted for them or for me.

"Addy is on her way up," Alexa said, rising from her chair. "I'm gonna go find Cope and help him get some coffees. He had to deal with the police questioning, but he's handled it, and they're gone now."

I couldn't nod, because my head felt like it weighed a million tons. "Thanks," I whispered. I didn't want Addy walking in here with Alexa sitting by my bedside. She didn't understand this world or what I had done.

I was going to have to come clean, though. If I'd died tonight, she wouldn't have known why. They would have never explained it to her. My secret would have died with me. Addy needed to know. She deserved to know.

I had to trust that she loved me enough to forgive me for all I'd done.

Alexa walked to the door, then stopped and looked back at me. "She got into a truck with Cope, a guy she'd never met, just because he told her you were in the hospital. She took a chance with her life because she was so worried about you. And we both know how Cope looks. She'll forgive anything." She headed out the door without another word.

They all knew my past with Addy now. I'd had to clue them in, but Cope had already researched her and knew everything. He'd even known Rose was Addy before I had. Bastard was a fucking genius.

The door had only been closed a few moments when it opened up again, and Addy came into the room, her eyes wide and her face flushed, like she'd been running.

"River," she said breathlessly. Then her hand covered her mouth, and she let out a small sob as she walked over to me slowly.

I wanted to get up and pull her into my arms, but I couldn't move.

"Come here," I said, using all my strength to lift my arm for her to come lie on my chest.

She didn't pause before doing exactly what I wanted.

I pressed a kiss to the top of her head. "I'm OK," I assured her.

"You were shot," she said on a choked sob.

This was why I had to tell her. She needed to know. I had

to face it, but at least it was done. I was done. This would never happen again. Benedetto had promised me that. "Yeah, but I'm going to be fine. I promise."

She sniffled. I hated that she had been crying. "What happened? Why weren't you at work? Or were you?"

When I'd gotten the text, I'd known I had to deal with this shit before it touched her or Franny. "I didn't go to work. At least, not the work you know. This was from before. The life I lived before I came to Rosemary Beach. The reason you couldn't find me for the last ten years."

She lifted her head off my chest and looked at me. Her eyes were full of concern. Telling her this was fucking terrifying. I didn't want her to walk away. Fact was, I'd chase her and beg her to stay if I needed to. But she had to know.

"It's a long story. Begins when I thought you were dead and I left my dad's. I was lost and homeless for a while, until I met a man. He gave me a home and a way to fight the pain and horror that consumed me. I want to tell you everything, but I'm fighting to stay awake on this medicine . . ." I didn't realize it until I said it, but suddenly, I was drowning in waves of drowsiness.

She reached up and ran her hand over my head, brushing my hair back gently. "Rest. I won't leave. I'm not leaving you."

My eyes drifted closed as she continued to play with my hair. "When I tell you . . . you might try. But I'll follow you," I said with a heavy tongue.

"Good," she replied, her words close to my ear.

Knowing she was there and not leaving was all I needed in that moment, and I let sleep pull me under.

. . .

When I opened my eyes again, I didn't have to look to find Addy. Her head was beside me, and her hand was tucked into mine as she slept. She was sitting on the chair she had pulled over next to the bed. I gazed down at her and enjoyed the view. She'd always been so peaceful when she slept. I loved watching her. Knowing she'd stayed close to me like this while I slept made me smile.

"She's been asleep for about an hour now." Blaire's voice startled me, and I turned my head to see my sister sitting on the other side of the bed, looking at me closely. "Major called Mase, who called Rush. Glad I got to hear it through the grapevine that my brother had been shot and was in the hospital." Now she looked annoyed.

"Guys I used to work with didn't know to call you," I told her.

She arched her eyebrows. "But they knew to call her?"

I glanced back down at her. "Yeah, they knew to call her."

Blaire let out a soft laugh so as not to disturb Addy. "I'd be hurt by that if I wasn't so happy to see someone as sweet and kind as her holding on to your hand like you were her entire world. I like seeing that."

She made everything right.

"You gonna tell her about this? About why you're in here?" Blaire asked. There was the flash of sisterly worry that I expected. But what exactly did she know about why I was in here?

"What do you mean?" I asked, watching her closely.

She leaned forward and held my gaze. "Do I look stupid to you? People do not just get shot in this town. Something else is happening here. You go away to Dallas and meet Mase and Reese. A man who deserves to die threatens Reese, then ends up dead himself. After that, you come here. I've thought about it, and something is off. You don't look or act like a man who wants to work in the restaurant business. You look like a man who knows how to handle a gun. So you getting shot in the leg doesn't add up with what you've been telling me. And just to be clear, you don't have to tell me anything. I just want you to know that I know something is up with you. Your past is sketchy. We don't know much about your adopted parents, and you don't talk about them. So yeah. Are you going to tell her the truth, at least?"

I nodded. Because I was, but that was all she would ever know.

Blaire smiled and stood up, then walked over to me and put her hand over my empty one. "Good. She's the one person who needs to know you. The real you. To make this work, you can't keep secrets. Trust me, I know."

"Thanks. I agree with you."

Blaire smiled and squeezed my hand. "If you need anything, call me. When you're ready, I want to bring Nate up here to visit. I'd stick around, but I think you have all the help you need, and you probably want some alone time with her, too."

"Yeah, I do," I said.

"It's going to be OK. She loves you," Blaire assured me, then turned and left the room.

Once she was gone, I turned my attention back to Addy as

she slept. It was morning now, and although I knew Addy well enough to know she had everything handled with Franny, I was still concerned about the girl waking up to her mom not being there.

Soon she'd have both of us there every morning. She would also have her own room, and I'd drive her to school every morning. I wanted to make up for all those years I'd lost with both mother and daughter.

Addy

I heard deep voices talking quietly as I slowly opened my eyes. I could feel the warmth of River's hand as it enclosed mine. I wasn't sure how long I'd been asleep, but when I woke up, I discovered his sister, Blaire, had been there. I'd never met her, but before River had figured out who I was, I had seen her visit the restaurant before.

Now it sounded like he had more visitors. I felt River's hand tighten over mine.

"Good morning," he said raspily.

I blinked and focused on him. "Hey," I replied, hoping I didn't look a mess.

His smile softened even more, and my heart did a little flutter in my chest. "You need to crawl up here beside me next time you sleep. You're going to be stiff and achy now."

I straightened up and stretched. "I'll be fine. You needed your sleep. I would have bothered you."

He shook his head. "No, you would have felt so damn good I would have probably slept longer."

I felt my cheeks warm, and I wanted to lean up and kiss him.

Someone cleared their throat behind me, and River's mouth

turned into a smirk as he lifted his eyes to the other people in the room. I'd forgotten they were there.

"Addy, I'd like you to meet some friends of mine," he said. I turned around, surprised to see a man with a woman beside him. Her long dark hair was in stark contrast to the bluest eyes I'd ever seen. She was holding the man's arm, and a kind smile was on her face. The bump under the sundress she was wearing made it easy to see that she was pregnant.

"Hello," I said, with a smile in her direction.

Her face broke into a pleased grin as she held out her free hand to me. "Hello, I'm Reese. It's so nice to meet you," she said, then turned her gaze back to the man beside her. "And this is my husband, Mase."

Husband. Oh, I liked that even better. River had married friends.

Mase was tall, with dark hair just long enough to keep pulled back in a low ponytail. His worn jeans fit him nicely, and the plaid button-down shirt he wore was long-sleeved, but he'd rolled them up to his elbows.

"Glad this one found a woman who can put up with him," Mase said.

My back stiffened, and my smile vanished. I decided I didn't like this Mase guy very much. "Excuse me?" I snapped, ready to defend my guy.

Reese laughed and hit Mase's arm. "Stop it before she takes a swing at you." She looked at me. "He's teasing. We're both very happy that Captain has found someone who cares about him like you obviously do. We want him happy."

Mase made a sound in his throat that sounded like he might not agree, but he didn't say more.

"You'll find I've got a colorful group of people in my world I call friends," River said from behind me.

I reached back and held on to his hand while studying these two so-called friends of his.

"Stop it, you two. She's going to hate us, and I want her to like us," Reese said with a worried frown. "These two didn't always see eye-to-eye on things, but in the end, they became friends. We live in Fort Worth, and the second we heard about his accident from Blaire, we got on a plane."

"His dad's private jet," River said with an amused tone.

Mase rolled his eyes, and Reese just smiled bigger. "OK, fine, it was a private jet, but we were in a hurry."

These two had a private jet? He looked like he belonged in Texas but not like he should have a private jet.

"Mase here is Kiro Manning's only son. He hates to admit it, but he is," River explained.

I knew that name, but who was it? I had heard it before. I just wasn't sure where.

Reese giggled and looked up at Mase. "See, she doesn't even know who Kiro is, so you're safe. No fangirling."

"Fangirling, my ass. Even when she realizes who he is, she won't be fangirling your ol' man," River said, sounding annoyed now.

I glanced back at River.

He grinned. "I fucking love that you don't know who Kiro is. You know that, right?"

Dangit, who was Kiro Manning?

"Slacker Demon, baby. His dad is Slacker Demon's lead singer."

That was when my jaw dropped. Because I might not remember the band members' names, but I sure as heck knew who Slacker Demon was. River squeezed my hand and frowned.

"His dad is in Slacker Demon?" I asked in a whisper, even though they could hear me.

"Yes, and he's not nearly as impressive as you're thinking," Mase replied.

"Yes, he is," Reese piped up.

I was slightly overwhelmed. How did River know these people?

"I own a ranch and raise horses. I'm not some damn rocker's kid." Mase sounded annoyed.

Reese patted his arm. "I know, baby. You're nothing like him."

"What the fuck ever," River said behind me. He was enjoying this, apparently.

"I think we've visited enough. Let's give Captain some rest, and we'll call to check in later. Rush and Blaire have been at us to visit for months, so we'll be there if you need anything," Reese said.

"Thanks. Appreciate it, but it's all good here. Give my nephew a hug for me," River said.

"Sure thing," Mase replied, and they left the room.

I turned back to River. "Wow, OK, that was interesting."

He sighed. "They're part of my past that I need to explain."

Captain

Mase had started to figure things out. I could see it in his eyes as he studied me. When I'd told them Addy was from my past and I'd loved her since I was a teenager, it had only enhanced his suspicions of why I'd been so focused on Reese before they married. He knew her father had something to do with the death of her stepfather, who had molested her. DeCarlo couldn't resist giving them a small hint.

But that was all Mase knew. Now I was sure he had started to piece together more of the puzzle. Which meant I had to talk to Addy before things blew up in my face and she heard the truth from somewhere else. I needed to be the one to explain it to her. Not that I had an excuse worth a damn. Killing someone was hard for anyone to accept. Even the lowest scum on earth.

Addy's heart and soul weren't wounded and broken the way mine had been when I thought I'd lost her. Trusting that she would forgive me and accept this was asking a lot. Losing her wasn't possible, either. Telling her the truth was my first step. I'd deal with the next step once I knew what that had to be.

"Do you like them?" she asked, breaking into my internal battle.

"Yeah, I do. He's a good man, and Reese is special. You'd love her if you got to know her. There's just so much they don't know about me that clouds their view of me. Things I want to explain to you. Things that scare the shit out of me to tell you, because I can't lose you."

Addy sat down in the chair she'd slept in and kept her nervous gaze locked on me. "This doesn't sound good," she said softly.

It *wasn't* good. It was dark and twisted and so completely fucked-up. But it was who I was and why I was here today. If I'd known for a moment that she was alive, I would have spent those years tracking her down. Searching for her. Saving her . . . and myself.

That wasn't how it had played out, though, and the past was something I couldn't change.

"I ran. I couldn't deal with the fact that you were gone. I hated everyone. Especially my dad, who never took the time to get my mom help. He left us there with her, and I thought she took your life. I was so angry and fucking empty." That was the easy part to tell.

Her hand came up and covered mine. That small touch helped some, but I wasn't sure she'd still touch me like that once she knew the whole truth.

"I lived on the streets for more than a year. I became good at it, or as good as you can be at living on your own at sixteen. One night, I decided to rip off a wealthy man. I normally spotted their wallets and got them without a hitch. I was fast. I didn't keep credit cards. I even destroyed them so no one could use them. I had some moral compass. But I did take the cash, just to keep myself fed. Made friends in the alleys so I could keep myself clothed." Stopping, I waited to see if she would comment. Stealing was the least of my sins. If she didn't accept that, then what I had to tell her was going to destroy me.

"Go on," she urged with a soft whisper.

"That night, I successfully took the wallet of Chicago's biggest crime lord. And he could have killed me. He had several men surrounding him, but I never even saw them until I took off running with his wallet, which he had no idea I'd swiped. But one of his guys did, and they stopped me. He couldn't believe I had his wallet, because he had felt nothing, but his guy pulled it from my coat pocket and tossed it to him. The man studied me for several moments. I knew by looking into his eyes that I was in trouble. There was power there that would terrify a normal person. But I had nothing to live for."

Her hand squeezed mine tightly, and I knew she didn't like hearing that. I picked her hand up and brought the back of it to my lips before continuing.

"He asked me my name and how old I was. Then he asked me how I felt about living on a boat. I didn't know what to say, so I was just honest and said it would be better than living in a box. So he took me home that night and gave me a place to live on his boat. Over the next year, he groomed me. Trained me. By the time I was eighteen years old, I was one of his. I observed his world, knowing that I wasn't OK with all of it. As soulless as I felt, I still had a heart. I couldn't condone it all, but I did see that he was operating in the areas where our judicial system failed."

I paused and prepared myself for what I still had to say. Addy was watching me closely. I didn't want to let her down. Telling her the truth was all I could do.

"I had one rule. A rule I never backed down from. I would only take the jobs when the mark was a man who had abused a child. That was all. No one else. Benedetto had become like the father I never had. He had given me shelter and a home when I needed it. I owed him. I also had demons clawing into my dreams and slowly eating me alive. I knew that what he was offering would be an outlet. A place to lose myself while finding a way to live again."

I stopped and watched her face. There was a slight frown on her lips as she sat quietly, still holding my hand. She didn't understand, but then, I hadn't been very detailed, either. The idea of actually saying I killed men seemed fucking impossible.

"What do you mean when you say a job and a mark?" she asked.

Addy wanted the details, and I had to give them to her.

"A job was someone Benedetto himself wanted gone or someone he'd been hired to off. A mark was the person who was to be . . . killed." Before I could freeze up, I continued. "I killed men, Addy. Many men. Each one of them had done terrible things to a child. I researched them. If I found them guilty, I ended their lives. That's how I know Reese. She was molested by her stepfather for years. He convinced her that she was stupid and dumb, when, in fact, she just had dyslexia and didn't know it. Her real father was the man who saved me. He wanted revenge, and I gave it to him. But he was only one of many. He was the last man I killed. After him, I ended it. I left Benedetto and started a new life. Here."

Addy's hand slipped from mine, and I let her move away. She needed space, and as much as it pained me, I had to respect that. I was prepared for this.

"You . . . killed people with a gun?" she asked in disbelief.

I nodded. "I killed monsters who repeatedly abused children."

She held her hands together in front of her and stared down at the ground. "How many?" she asked quietly.

I wanted to tell her I didn't know or that it wasn't a lot. But the fact was, I knew every face. I remembered every moment of the ends of their lives. "Twenty-six," I replied.

"Twenty-six," she repeated, as if she was trying to let it sink in. "If you stopped, why did you get shot?"

"Members of a gang that one of my marks was in wanted revenge and tracked me down. Those who still work for Benedetto were trailing them here. That's why Alexa is here, and that's how I know her. Cope, too. When they had them in sight, it was my job to go end it. Either I killed them, or they killed me. I killed two of them, and Cope killed one. The last one went down with his finger on the trigger, and the bullet went through my leg."

She took several steps back until she was leaning against the wall, staring at me.

I wanted to know what she was thinking. The look of revulsion I had feared wasn't on her face, but she wasn't OK with this. I could tell that much. But then, I hadn't expected her to be.

"Will others track you down?"

I shook my head no. "That was an unusual situation. Most don't know who did the job. The gang knew because of their dealings with Benedetto in the past."

She ran a hand through her hair nervously. "You could have died."

"No, I couldn't have. I went in with backup, and I had a gun. I'm a professional. I was safe."

"A professional killer?"

That was what I didn't want her to think. "That's not what I meant. I knew what I was doing. I was safe."

"What if more come? What if they hurt Franny?" She covered her mouth and shook her head, as if the idea had just hit her.

I sat up, wincing at the pain in my leg, wishing like hell I could pull her into my arms to reassure her. "No one will ever touch Franny or you. I'd never let it happen. You're my life, Addy. The two of you are my life."

Addy backed away, moving to the door. "I can't," she said, shaking her head no. "I just can't." Then she spun around and ran out the door.

I couldn't move. She'd left me, and I couldn't fucking move to go after her.

Addy

He killed people.

I stood in the kitchen, staring outside, with a cup of coffee in my hand, that simple fact running through my head. Franny was safely at school, and I needed sleep, but I wasn't sure that would ever come again.

I loved him.

That was the other thing I couldn't get out of my head. I loved him, even still. Maybe more. How screwed-up did that make me? How could I love him more for killing people? Because they were scum who abused kids? Did that make it OK? In my heart, it did. I wanted perverts who ruined kids' lives to die. Just thinking of someone hurting Franny that way made me furious. If someone were to abuse her, I'd kill him myself.

So did that make me any different?

He told me the truth when he didn't have to. That was something he never had to tell me. He could have lied to me. He could have made up a story that made sense. Telling me the truth had been big. Huge, even. Which made me love him even more.

I was still sorting it all out. I'd run away from the hospital shortly after River had finished his story. All I'd been able to see was Franny's face in the moment. The fear that his life choices could hurt her had been too much. She wanted him in our life as much as I did, but at what cost could I let that happen?

Was he right that this was it? No more backlash from his past could threaten him and potentially threaten our daughter? I wanted to believe that and move on, but she was my first priority. She needed me to protect her. Being selfish because I loved River so much I couldn't breathe wasn't acceptable. I had to do what was best for her.

But being near her father felt right. I wanted it to be right. To be safe. And I wanted to trust him to keep her safe.

I wanted her to have everything. Stability. A father.

I had wanted River most of my life. He had gotten lost and found a way to survive, and as much as I didn't support what he had done, it didn't change the fact that I loved him. I would always love him.

I set my coffee cup down on the counter. I knew what I was going to do. I either had to own this or run from it. I'd never run from anything before. Except when I was trying to save River's life.

This time, I wanted to give all three of us the life that had been stolen from us. I had that in my power now. I wasn't a scared teenage girl with no one to turn to. I was tough. I'd learned to survive on my own, and I had made it.

It was time I stopped being scared.

Two hours later, I had Franny with me, and we walked to River's hospital room. I'd explained to her that he had been shot

in the leg by accident, and he was going to be fine. She'd panicked, of course, but I'd calmed her down. Then she'd made
me go to the store and get him a bag of chocolate kisses, a box
of doughnuts, a bag of chips, and two Get Well balloons. This
was apparently what she felt everyone needed to feel better.

"Do you think he'll be awake?" she asked, as we made our
way down the hall toward his room.

"I don't know, but we will wait for him quietly if he's sleeping," I assured her, because I knew that once we got in, she
wasn't going to want to leave.

When we got close to the door, I heard a woman's voice,
and she sounded upset. I paused, not sure I wanted to take
Franny in just yet.

"Someone is in there, Mommy," Franny said, looking up at
me, concerned.

"I bet it's his sister, Blaire. Maybe we should wait—"

"You can't leave," I heard. "Stop being so stubborn! I'll call
her. I'll get her up here. You can't even walk, Captain." Blaire's
voice had risen so that her words were crystal-clear. Unmistak-
able.

He was trying to leave because of me. I reached for Franny's hand and hurried her toward the room with me. He didn't
need to move. I just hoped he hadn't tried yet. I wouldn't be
able to forgive myself if he made his injury worse.

"I'm leaving this fucking hospital and—" His words stopped
when he saw Franny and me. He took us both in, along with
the items we held in our arms.

"Hey," Franny said, sounding nervous. "I don't think you
need to get up. You'll hurt your leg worse. Tell him, Mommy.
He can't get up."

She'd heard enough of the distress in Blaire's voice to know he was about to do something stupid. Beautifully perfect but stupid.

"Lie back down, River. Please," I said, walking over to set the items I was holding down on the table before going to him. "We're back. We aren't leaving."

He looked hopeful as he watched me.

"Thank God," Blaire said, sounding relieved. "As much as I want to meet Franny and have some family bonding time, I think this family needs some time alone."

"Yeah," River agreed, not looking back at his sister.

"Thanks, Blaire, and I'm sorry about that," I told her, knowing she'd understand what I meant. I didn't want to say too much in front of Franny.

"I got you balloons. Well, Mommy got them, too. And we got you good stuff to eat 'cause hospital food is gross. Why were you leaving? Was it because the food was gross?"

Her questions brought a smile to the corners of River's mouth. "The food is bad, but if you've brought me the good stuff, then I reckon I can relax and stay here a while longer."

Franny beamed at him and started pulling out the doughnuts to put in front of him. "We didn't bring milk, because Mommy said they'd have that here. You need milk with doughnuts."

"I agree completely. We need to get us each a glass of milk and open this box up."

I wasn't sure he could eat anything like doughnuts yet, but I'd deal with that when the nurses came. He was going to tell Franny anything she wanted to hear at this point, and I loved him even more for that. She was doing a good job of not showing how upset she was over seeing him in that bed, with his leg all bandaged up and hanging there.

He turned to look at me, so softly that I felt I might melt. "You came back."

I nodded. "Yeah. I left something here that I love."

His eyes crinkled at the corners as his smile grew. "Yeah?"

"Yeah," I replied.

"Then you think you can love it with the past that comes with it?"

I shrugged and stepped closer to him. "I've loved it for most of my life. Can't stop now."

River held out a hand to me, and I slipped mine into his. He pulled me closer, and I went willingly.

"Wait . . . do you love Mommy?" Franny's tone was a mix of awe and excitement.

"Loved her since she was twelve years old. Never stopped," he replied.

The warmth of his words spread through me, and I leaned into him.

"Does this mean you're gonna marry her?" Franny asked, clasping her hands together, with wide eyes as she looked at us.

"That's not—" I started to say, but was cut off when River pulled me down for a quick, chaste kiss.

"Yeah, if she'll have me. It'd make me the luckiest man on the planet to have both of you in my life, together."

Smiling against his lips, I turned my head to see Franny watching us with a hopeful expression. "I think it's safe to say we both love you and want to keep you."

She nodded her head enthusiastically. "Yes, we will marry you!" she exclaimed.

Captain chuckled and held out his other hand toward her.

She ran over to him and was careful not to hurt him as she let him pull her to his side.

"Got my girls," he said, kissing the top of her head. "Makes all the paths I took to get me here worth every last mile."

Franny didn't understand the depth of that, but I did. One day, she would, too.

Acknowledgments

Writing a book is challenging. Writing a book without support is impossible. There are so many who deserve my gratitude.

I need to begin with my children: Austin, Annabelle, and Ava. They are the ones closest to me. The ones who deal with Mom being locked away in her office. They give a lot toward every book I write.

My editor, Jhanteigh Kupihea, for putting up with my missed deadlines and forgetfulness. She helps make my books the best they can be. I'd be lost without her.

Ariele Fredman, Judith Curr, and the rest of the team at Atria for being the support I need to put my books out there.

Jane Dystel, my amazing badass agent, who I love. Choosing her is one of the best decisions I've made in my journey. Lauren Abramo, for handling all my foreign sales.

Monica Tucker. If she didn't keep up with me, I'd be in a mess! She keeps my bills paid, food in my pantry, emails answered, and a multitude of other things.

Abbi's Army, a group of readers who support me, promote me, and make me feel loved, even on my worst days. I love y'all!!

Every person who has ever bought one of my books. Thank you. I get to do what I love most in the world because of you.